T0319204

Zimbabwe:
The Urgency of Now

Tendai R. Mwanaka

Langaa Research & Publishing CIG
Mankon, Bamenda

Publisher:
Langaa RPCIG
Langaa Research & Publishing Common Initiative Group
P.O. Box 902 Mankon
Bamenda
North West Region
Cameroon
Langaagrp@gmail.com
www.langaa-rpcig.net

Distributed in and outside N. America by African Books Collective
orders@africanbookscollective.com
www.africanbookscollective.com

ISBN: 9956-792-34-9

DISCLAIMER
All views expressed in this publication are those of the author and do not
necessarily reflect the views of Langaa RPCIG.

Table of Contents

Acronyms

AIPPA	Access to Information Protection and Privacy Act
ANC	African National Congress
AU	African Union
CIO	Central Intelligence Organisation
DFC	The Defence Forces Commission
DSC	Defence and Security Commission
FRELIMO	The Mozambique Liberation Front
GNU	Government of National Union
GPA	Global Political Agreements
JOC	Joint Operations Command
JOMIC	Joint Monitoring and Implementation Committee
MDC-N	Movement for Democratic Change-Ncube
MDC	Movement for Democratic Change
MDC-T	Movement for Democratic Change-Tsvangirai
NCA	National Consultative Assembly
NDSS	National Defence and Security Strategy
NGO	Non-Governmental Organisation
POSA	Public Order Security Act
SADC	Southern African Development Community
SSR	Security Sector Reforms
SWAPO	South West African People's Organisation
UNIP	United National Independence Party
ZACRO	Zimbabwe Association for Crime Prevention and Rehabilitation of the Offender
ZANU-PF	Zimbabwe African National Union Patriotic Front
ZBC	Zimbabwe Broadcasting Corporation
ZDF	Zimbabwe Defence Forces
ZEC	Zimbabwe Electoral Commission
ZESN	Zimbabwe Election Support Network
ZNLWVA	Zimbabwe National Liberation War Veterans Association
ZPS	Zimbabwe Prison Service

ZRP   Zimbabwe Republic Police

N.B. The acronym MDC will be used in this book for MDC-T, or all the MDCs combined together if the issues apply to all the camps. Where I focus on the other camps I will use their specific acronyms.

Chapter 1

Prologue

Zimbabwe: The Urgency of Now is a collection of creative nonfiction pieces. It is a follow-up to ZIMBABWE: THE BLAME GAME (Tendai R Mwanaka, 2013). With *Zimbabwe: The Urgency of Now*, I focused on Zimbabwe political, economic and social landscape post the negotiations of the government of national unity(*6th Year of Zim Talks*), the GNU years (*GNU Entity and Power-sharing Deal Limitations*), the 2013 July elections (*2013 Elections Preparedness*), and post 2013 elections (*Post-election Zimbabwe's Political, Economic and Social Landscape*). The intentions of this book are to discover the real problems and proffer solutions to the problems. For a lot of us, we are still trying to figure out what to think of, and do after the 2013 elections, and the particular essay, *Post-election Zimbabwe's Political, Economic and Social Landscape* focuses on this for me, and for everyone else. I am trying to understand what to do, or what the country could do.

But for the country to keep on the track of being a multi-party democracy based on social justice and equality before the law, we need to keep the opposition relevant in Zimbabwe's political landscape, that's why I have decided it to be the focus of the book. I have a number of essays that deal with the opposition politics, especially the main MDC lead by Morgan Tsvangirai. Yes, I am not a fan of the ZANU-PF party, but in this book, it's not supposed to be a hate book against the ZANU-PF, but of its hegemony over our political landscape. I don't think it's healthy for the country to have ZANU-PF, 34 years down the line, with all that it has done to destroy our country, still getting over two thirds of the plebiscite vote. Considering we had come to half-half share of the plebiscite

1

vote in the 2008 elections, I find something simply wrong with what and where we are at now.

The problem why we are here lies with the two players in our country, ZANU-PF and the MDC, and these I try to focus on, especially the MDC-T. I think it is because of the MDC that we are now here, and it is now evident with the troubles engulfing the party again, as it totters on the brink of the breakup, with two new camps, one headed by the founder and president of this party, Morgan Tsvangirai, and the other camp by Tendai Biti. I said the troubles engulfing the party again because I want to focus on the latest upheavals in the MDC-T. There have been breakups before, the 2005 breakup that ushered the Welshman Ncube lead MDC, and later Job Sikala and Munyaradzi Gwisai broke out from this MDC-N to form their own MDCs-but Job Sikala is now back in the MDC-T

The fighting lies in the top echelons of the MDC but the problems roots down into the cells and structures where the party has lost contact with its supporters. The two heads of these camps, it's obvious, have failed us. It's these two camps that made the party to be incapable to gear up to the last election. I have to clarify; I am talking of the camps that become very visible as we toward the elections. Readers shouldn't confuse the camps to mean after the break-up that has now happened after elections that is now obtaining. I wrote the book before the breakup became official. It is not farfetched to assume the dreaded CIO is involved in this project to break the opposition party, like they were involved in the 2005 breakup, and it's now a matter of time. But in *The Urgency of Now*, I try to be hopeful that sense would prevail and that these camps would solve their problems.

The ZANU-PF, as usual, has its own camps, the usually touted Mnangagwa-Mujuru camps, some even furthering up saying three camps, including Mugabe's camp, but I would like to think it is two camps, with Mugabe playing around both camps, balancing them and staying the ZANU-PF from open warfare between the protagonists. These camps, with the death of Mugabe, could really be explosive, even pushing the country into a war situation. Mujuru versus Mnangagwa camp fight right down into the government structures such as the police, army, CIO etc... The Mujuru camp has control over the Mashonaland and Manicaland Provinces, and the Mnangagwa camp has control over the Midlands, Masvingo, and Matabeleland Provinces and there is that threat for the fight to be along those provincial lines. But in this book, it's not an immediate problem. If the ZANU-PF manages its affairs well, if Mugabe can find a successor now who would be accepted by the party there won't be any problem in this party. It has a lot of leaders who could be possible replacements to Mugabe, anytime. Mugabe has been creating a lot of successors, rather than one successor as we supposed he should be doing. Jonathan Moyo, Didymus Mutasa, Emerson Mnangagwa, Joyce Mujuru, Constantine Chiwengwa, Sidney Sekeramayi, Patrick Chinamasa, Rugare Gumbo, Simon Khaya Moyo, Gideon Gono etc..., are all capable leaders to take over. The problem is there is no one anointed heir to the throne, and Mugabe needs to sort-out that problem, as soon as possible.

Unlike the ZANU-PF, which is awash with alternatives, the MDC has not much to go for. The MDC has always been about Morgan Tsvangirai and nobody else. I need to explain why I think the MDC has been all about Tsvangirai, yet someone might point out the same applies across the ZANU-PF, where everything has been about Mugabe. The advantage the ZANU-PF has over the MDC over this issue is the ZANU-PF has had over 34 years in government in which the above leaders have been offered opportunities to lead several ministries and departments thus garnering experience of governance, as well as creating clout (cultish), in their own right. I will give an example; Didymus Mutasa is known to have great control of the Manicaland Province, Mujuru of the Mashonaland, Mnangagwa of the Midlands, Sekeramayi and

Chiwengwa of the army, Gono of the financial institutions, Chinamasa of the Judiciary, Jonathan Moyo of the media etc., which is lacking in Tsvangirai's possible replacements. It's only Tsvangirai who has this kind of clout. He is also the one who draws the votes in this party, and in this book, I try to figure-out whether there are suitable alternatives and analyse these alternatives.

We have always had the problem of our army and security sector involving themselves with the political processes, and I have two particular essays that deal with this, *Security Sector Reforms*, and *Recommendations on Security Sector Reforms*. As you have noted above, I included the army boss, Constantine Chiwengwa, as one of the contenders to the ZANU-PF throne. We have the army still involved in political process and it would be short-sighted to rule them out. With that understanding, in the essays I try to figure out how to prise the army's grip off our political processes; how to do reforms so that our security sector would start focussing on its real mandates.

The other clutch of essays deals with issues to do with Africa, problems that are hampering movements towards the creation of the United States of Africa. I have always believed in this dream but it's always bogged down, by our politicians. I am trying to figure out how we can take it back into strides, and what it would solve. Another essay that doesn't deal particularly with Zimbabwe is *Towards Malemanialess in the Land Reform in South Africa*. It's the hugest threat to security and economic development for South Africa, the land reform being articulated by Julius Malema, and I am trying to figure out how they could pre-empty that threat, especially how the whites could start the land reform themselves without waiting for the government.

The last clutch of essays looks at our psyche, Zimbabweans' psyche, i.e., *The Lost Dream, The Strike Years, Conditioned to Fear, Unlearning Fear and the Shadow That Refused to*

Leave. I am trying to understand the Zimbabweans; their thinking now, what has stopped them from realising a dream that was shining on the horizons, some few years ago.

Like in *Zimbabwe: The Blame Game*, I have tried to free myself from fetters of academic, or journalistic type of nonfiction writing and have experimented with the creative nonfiction type of writing, where I look at the issues in a creatively focussed, laidback, imaginative, simple language, with the story-telling genre, diary, memoirs, playwriting and poetic genre being mixed with nonfiction. My intention is still to attract the general readers who might not want to deal with unnecessary jargon and sophistication of the academic genre.

Chapter 2

6th Year of Zim Talks

AU Election Body: The elections were not free and fair.

AU meeting, Egypt: So we all agree the presidential election was not free and fair. We kindly ask his Excellency, the president of Zimbabwe to engage the MDC in negotiations with the intention of forming a government of national unity, with facilitation of his Excellency, president Mbeki.

One month later:

Uncle Bob: What really worries you, my prime minister?

Chematama: A snare, I think a lovely snare. I can feel the signal.

Uncle Bob: But, you will be my prime minister.

Chematama: With what powers?

Hwenyakwese: My friend, let's laugh whilst this lasts. Uncle Bob has been very generous to us, don't you see that! You will be the prime minister, and I will be your vice-prime minister with the home affairs portfolio. You really don't have to worry about Uncle Bob but rather you should be wary of that old schemer, the other vice-prime minister with the defence portfolio. That one is the real snake in the grass. I don't want him in my council of ministers, in fact in our council of ministers, but let's sign this deal before Uncle Bob changes his mind, my friend.

7

Chematama: Don't you see, young fool, that it's a trap; he has sweetened our cakes with stupid posts.

Hwenyakwese: Then cut the cake and let's all celebrate my friend.

Chematama: Let me go and think about that and consult with my party
(*Chematama exits*).

Uncle Bob: I have always told you that he is a sell-out. He is going to consult with that McGee American ambassador.

Mbeki: (*addressing journalists*). Our prime minister has asked for some time to consult. I have always told you the best solutions would come from the Zimbabweans themselves, and I expect a deal to be signed in the next 24 hours.

Zimbabwean: When will they sign that bloody deal? We are so sick and tired of hearing the same promises everyday.

Zimbabwean: Let's give thanks to our African brother Thabo for he has done a great job to bring them to negotiations. Didn't you see they even shook hands, a couple of weeks ago?

Zimbabwean: What shaking of hands! Mbeki is a traitor. He is the old boy's friend. Don't expect any deal any sooner.

Zimbabwean: I wonder where I could find food to eat today. I last ate three days ago. I wish Uncle Bob, Chematama, and Hwenyakwese could really be eaten.

2 days later:

Vavi: SADC shouldn't invite Mad Bob and that ladies lover kanga-man from that small mountain kingdom country to come. We are going to strike like nobody has ever seen if these dictators come to their SADC talkathon thing. We are going to bring Johannesburg to a standstill.

Malema: Yes comrade! We will kill for Uncle Bob, but if that white kangaroo human rights organisation refuses us the opportunity to kill for Uncle Bob, then we might as well kill for Mswati, you see...

At the SADC meeting:

Mbeki: Gentleman and gentle ladies we have negotiated a settlement for Zimbabwe and what's left is the signing ceremony. But, I want to ask you fellow leaders to tell Tsvangirai to sign it.
(*Uncle Bob nodes his head and smiles in agreement with Mbeki*).

SADC: You have got to sign this deal or else we won't allow you to stay in Southern Africa, or even to visit our countries, in fact we will deport you to Britain, like what old-man Mbeki here is doing to your fellows caught in the cyclone Xenophobia.

Chematama: I will not sign it unless if I am given significant executive powers to curb Mad Bob's excessive irrationalities. I also do not want to report to Mad Bob, but to parliament for starters.
(*He leaves the meeting*).

Hwenyakwese: He wants all the powers to himself so what power-sharing deal would that be if he takes all of good

9

Uncle Bob's powers? Too bad, I have to go back to Zimbabwe without anything but, for him to take all of Uncle's powers? No!

Mbeki: I thought he would be pressured to sign but it seems not. That's the best deal I had negotiated from my best friend. It was really a good beginning, but I have to start all over talking to that old wiser again. It's something I don't want to do again. He should simply have signed it, but, maybe he doesn't know how to sign it, after all that fellow is not educated, but he signed that other hoodwink paper in Harare, didn't he? The wine is wasting away in that beautiful Harare hotel where I enjoyed spending the best part of this year in. Such a waste! But, of course..., let's give him some time to reconsider. The best deal lies with the Zimbabweans....

Uncle Bob: Time is not what I have friend. Those Brishit browns and damn American bushes are pounding at my front door, back door, roof and all the windows. Very soon they will take me to that damn American Security Council thing and their crime war court thing, you know that friend!

Mbeki: Don't worry my friend. Remember we still have our Russian and Chinese friends. You know that with Vietnam and that other poor African country, the five of us will block those imperialist British and Americans until god-knows when.

Uncle Bob: Thanks old boy. I will give you another farm next time you make your frequent visits to my beloved country. You know Zimbabwe is mine. I was given that country by our spirit mediums Mbuya Kaguvi and Sekuru Nehanda. No, no, no, it must be the other way round, that is, Sekuru Kaguvi and Mbuya Nehanda. But, my friend, you can do that lie-thing of yours to those Brishit newsman over there. I wish Blair was still there. It had been so easier to out-fox him all those years because he talked too much and didn't do anything of whatever he could have said. He was like those Blair toilets we have in my country, so smelly. (*They laugh*). But, with this Brown thing, I am so scared of him. Don't you see that even the Brishit themselves are as scared of him as I am? (*He chuckles*). And that warmongering son-of-a-bitch, "Shoes" Bush, no-o, no, no, no…I don't want him on my back, no my friend!

Mbeki: Don't worry, friend! (*Addressing journalists*). We will continue negotiating and a deal is very likely in the next day or so, and as I have always told you it must be the Zimbabweans who should decide their destiny and the deal they want, so negotiations will be continuing.

Zimbabwean: So what does that mean?

Zimbabwean: I don't know, maybe it means other 5 years with the old Mad Bob, again?

Zimbabwean: iiii,uhiii,uuu

Zimbabwean: …….

I wrote this part-play, part-humour take on Zimbabwe's political situation, and especially the early days of the power-sharing negotiations in 2008 when the negotiations started. I included it in this book, especially at the start of the book because I think it was the early attitudes of the players in the negotiations that ultimately cut the deal for each player. And it was this deal that shaped the politics of Zimbabwe during the GNU entity and now, post GNU Zimbabwe. The oncoming topic deals with the nitty-gritty of the GNU, its limitations, so this chapter serves as an introductory note of this topic

Chapter 3

GNU Entity and Power-Sharing Deal Limitations

The year 2008 goes down in history as the year in which the people of Kenya and Zimbabwe were deprived of their right to choose political leaders of their choice, as enshrined under Article 21 of the Universal Declaration of Human and People's Rights (1948) and Article 13 of the African Charter on Human and People's Right (1986), both of which state that "Every citizen shall have the right to participate freely in the government of his country, either directly or through freely chosen representatives in accordance with the provisions of the law"(UDHPR,1948; ACHPR,1986). The politically-motivated violence, which followed these elections, if it is anything to go by, flies on the face of this freedom to people's right to choose political leaders of their choice. GOVERNMENT OF NATIONAL UNITY (GNU) AS A CONFLICT PREVENTION STRATEGY: CASE OF ZIMBABWE AND KENYA. By Jephias Mapuva (African Centre for Citizenship and Democracy [ACCEDE] School of Government, University of the Western Cape, South Africa. Journal of Sustainable Development in Africa (Volume 12, No.6, 2010: 250-251).

The problems of Zimbabwe goes a long way back from independence, somehow it's always the one who has power, but not the absolute majority, who has the strength to push through their needs in any negotiation. *"Abayiwa ngaabude"* is the Shona aphorism that estimates what I am trying to allude to. In hunting, the most precious animal one could catch was a pangolin, which was exclusively for the kings. But, for one to capture the pangolin they had to content with its piercing arrows, which it would release onto your face when you try to

13

capture it. Its either you had to deal with these arrows and get your pangolin or run away from these arrows and loose the opportunity to capture this king's bounty. If you capture this pangolin, and when you give it to the king, you would receive a lot of gifts; land, cattle, etc... *Abayiwa ngaabude*, means you either have to accede to the pain of the arrows and abandon this game of co-existence, or you have to adapt to those arrows and make do with what's there, for the ultimate prize. This has always been the situation with Zimbabwe. You either have to adapt well to the arrows of those already in power, for you to capture power for yourself. And, it is those inside who have the biggest say. Jephias Mapuva (2010:251) developing his augment from (Beetham, 1999) observes that;

> The prevailing practice has been that in many post-colonial African countries, there has been dominance by rulers inclined to share power only with a very small coterie of collaborators.

After Zimbabwe's independence, the whites, even though they didn't have the majority support, used their power to curve out a deal that protected them and their interests. The problem was the liberation was not won by the sword. There was no decisive defeat of the Rhodesians by the liberators, such that the liberators were forced to negotiate with little power. Mugabe and the ZANU-PF understood this phenomenon, and ever since that, Mugabe has used that to stay in power, as well.

Mugabe has used the power he had because he was an insider to create or curve out a deal he wanted for himself and his party. He did that with the 2008 negotiations that ushered the GNU entity. He got all the powerful ministries (defence, security, core leadership in home affairs, foreign affairs, agriculture, justice, mining), and the MDC was left to content with powerless social and economic ministries, maybe except for the finance ministry that had a bit of clout. I feel it's the only ministry that the MDC had good control over, maybe through the sheer personality of Tendai Biti who was the minister there, and all the other ministries, even though the MDC had the minister, the rest of the staffers were ZANU-PF people, so that not much change happened in those ministries. The situation was such that the MDC failed to change the makeup of those ministries, so power stayed with ZANU-PF.

Even the prime minister, Morgan Tsvangirai was more or less a ceremonial prime minister, because he reported to the president, rather than to report to the parliament. He didn't have power over the cabinet, so whatever policies that had to be formulated for governance were under direct control of the president. Somehow Tsvangirai was a mere manager who reported to the director in the running, day to day running, of the government. He couldn't even stamp his authority as the prime minister on ministers from the ZANU-PF, because they were not answerable to him. He had the position that had little control over the ministries that the ZANU-PF controlled. In being powerless, in feeling that he was powerless, he wasted most of his time in trying to fight cabinet wars, using his ministers to do the camp fighting, whereby they would cut back on any ZANU-PF policies, or policies coming from the ministries that ZANU-PF controlled, through ministries they controlled.

The term "government of national unity" is a term used to refer to a case in which all the major political parties in a country are part of the governing coalition. By nature, these GNUs are a fragile, acrimonious, usually transitional arrangement with a high risk of disintegrating at the slightest opportunity and further degenerating into conflict. For the 5 years of the GNU, it was always fragile, with accusations being flighted, left and right, and Nelson Chamisa almost resigned from his ministry when some of his portfolio in ITC was removed by the president and transferred to the minister of

Transport and communication, Nicolas Goche, who is from the ZANU-PF. Not to talk of other points of disagreements on the swearing in of the minister of agriculture, Roy Bennet (MDC), whom Mugabe refused to swear in, saying he still was facing prosecution charges. When he was acquitted the president still was reluctant such that the MDC ended up fielding another cadre, and Bennet returned to his exile base in South Africa, still necessitating the MDC to work with a fractured and dispersed house. There were also disagreements on the Reserve Bank Governor, Gideon Gono whom the MDC wanted out, also on the Attorney General, Tomana, the balancing and sharing of permanent secretaries, provincial governors and ambassadors.

The other example is of the Chisumbanje Ethanol Plant that the minister directly responsible, Elias Mangoma, it seemed, from the ZANU-PF controlled public broadcaster ZBC's reports, was scuppering, because it had been initiated by the ZANU-PF party before the GNU entity. And, the ZANU-PF milked this in these public media, to their benefit, telling the people it was the MDC which was scuppering the people's chances for employment, of electricity and fuel security and upliftment.

There were a lot other battles that the MDC concentrated on, in trying to piss the ZANU-PF because of this lack of power that they had in the entity, which ZANU-PF used to create sympathy with the electorate, through its mouth piece, the ZBC. Whilst the MDC was concentrating on trying to fight this redundancy in the GNU, the ZANU-PF was doing its usual thing, campaigning for the forthcoming elections. If you watched the public media pre-2008, you would notice there were no changes in post-GNU, whatsoever, in terms of coverage and policy shifts on the public media towards the two parties? The ZBC continued giving time to the ZANU-PF in its programmes, just like it did prior-2008, and very little, progressive issues of the MDC, found their way into these media. So, the ZANU-PF had those 5 years of the GNU campaigning, whilst the MDC was concentrating on negotiations.

The ZANU-PF created every diversion it could think of, and the MDC, like a starved dog, chased every bone the ZANU-PF threw at it, and ZANU-PF enmeshed the MDC into fighting for power through negotiations, throughout the GNU entity. The ZANU-PF could stick on any issue, like for instance, adoption of the constitution, for weeks on end, and whilst the MDC was pushing for the adoption of the constitution, putting diplomatic pressure through their negotiators, the ZANU-PF stuck on its positions, making absolutely crazy conditions, created a lot of hullabaloo in its public media. Yet, in the same media, it was fully campaigning, using every sticking point to point out the MDC's unsuitability and incapability to take over the government. Whilst the likes of Tsvangirai, Biti, Welshmen Ncube, Arthur Mutambara etc… were focusing on making the GNU entity work, the ZANU-PF didn't care whether it worked or not, and thus created stumbling blocks for it, but went back to connect with the electorate.

The MDC grassroots leaders lost sight of their electorate, and concentrated on the negotiations, thinking that if they get a better deal through the negotiations they would have an election that was free and fair, and win the election. They lost touch with the electorate, whilst grassroots ZANU-PF people went down into the villages, into cells, into wards, into provinces, creating a relationship again with the electorate. The MDC leadership was concentrating on the negotiations, crying pell-mell, in foreign media, and in the few private media in Zimbabwe.

I will give an example of me, and my ward or constituency. All through the last 5 years of the GNU, I never saw the MDC MP I voted for, or heard he was in our local ward doing something, some project for the constituency. I suppose they were concentrating on enriching themselves. The state's job is the most valuable prize in African politics. The state power can be used to create opportunities for private gain. Where private sector opportunities are limited, the occupation of public office remains the most reliable means of accumulating wealth, through awarding of tenders and contracts for government jobs. Ibbo Mandaza lays out this logic in Zimbabwean context:

> ...The quest for power and wealth expressed itself sometimes in open corruption and nepotism. The long years of colonial domination and deprivation, not to mention imprisonment and the hard days of the struggle, became almost the licence – albeit for only a few among the many who might claim such a licence – to accumulate quickly; and the state ...appeared the most viable agency for such accumulation (Mandaza 1986, 56-57).

So that, despite even the fact that our MP had been set aside money for the constituency development, up to now, I don't know what he did with that allocation. I never saw the local ward councillor, I never saw anyone from the MDC at my place, trying to get my vote, yet there are at least three grassroots MDC leaders in my small street, Svosve Street. They just assumed because I was young, and I stayed in town, and I understood the politics of the country; that I knew how ZANU-PF had messed the country, and that automatically, I would vote for the MDC. To tell the truth, I still voted for it, even with all these glaring mistakes. Furthermore, nobody from the MDC has ever approached me to join the party, even though I wouldn't accept, but I have had to deal with a lot of ZANU-PF grassroots supporters trying to get my vote, trying to entice me into the ZANU-PF structures.

So, if the GNU was the beast that consumed the MDC, these questions beg. Was it worth it to enter the power-sharing negotiations and the GNU entity? Was that the right move for the MDC, back then? Mapuva developing his argument from (Maunganidze, 2009) posit that

> While there is no doubt that effective unity is desirable, especially in furtherance of democracy, it could be argued that the kind of unity that we are seeing being emerged in Kenya and Zimbabwe may actually herald the corrosion of democracy as we have come to know it, where the elite unites to further their own interests and not those of the nation (p. 251).

In agreement with Maunganidze and Mapuva, I would repeat my position, which I stated in the essay, THE POINT OF CONTENTION: THE POLICE, in the nonfiction book, ZIMBABWE: THE BLAME GAME (Tendai R Mwanaka, 2013). The MDC should have stayed out of it, or if they had entered the negotiations, they should have only agreed to a deal that gave them real power, power to change the course of our destiny, power to change this democracy for the best.

In their paper, THE ANATOMY OF POLITICAL PREDATION (2011, Executive Summary: 5) Michael Bratton and Eldred Masunungure say,

> In practice, the GNU has been unable to implement the central provisions of the GPA, leading to repeated breakdowns in communication and cooperation between President and Prime Minister. The roots of the impasse lie in the Mugabe's unwillingness to share power and resistance to political reform by senior military elements in the dominant coalition. But the divisions, inexperience and organizational weaknesses of the rival MDC coalition are also to blame.

This is echoed by Mapuva (2010: 254) who says,

> James Hamill (2008) has put forward three principal objections to the national unity argument as it was currently being advanced for Zimbabwe. First, Hamill asserts that a GNU impedes attempts to entrench democratic values on the continent - integral to which is the absolute necessity that parties (and governments) accept election defeat and orderly transfers of power. National unity is invariably couched in a noble rhetoric, but in reality it indulges those who are prepared to unleash terror and mayhem to impose themselves upon the people and secure in the knowledge, that, at the very least, they will have carved out a continuing role for themselves in the government by so doing. That is entirely incompatible with the democratic principles, which African states and African multilateral organisations have claimed to embrace since 2000. It has been pointed out that the paradox of the national unity governments is that they rarely produce national unity and certainly will not do so in Zimbabwe, against the backdrop of the huge citizen dissatisfaction.

But MDC leadership accepted this vacuous deal from the ZANU-PF. It should have stayed out without a good deal from these negotiations. It was outside the governance of the country, so there was no governance obligation from them. Mapuva (2010: 253) posits,

> While GNUs are appropriate in countries like Kenya where there are many ethnic groups, in Zimbabwe, the concept is inappropriate due to the monolithic demographic pattern where any elected leader would be able to unite the nation.

Knox Chitiyo in his book, *The Case for Security Sector Reform in Zimbabwe*, arguing on security sector reforms, felt the two parties to the dispute, didn't have a *Shared Vision*, saying,

> The three parties lack a mutual vision of where they want Zimbabwe to go. There is an emergent and valuable symmetry regarding the process, but there is a fundamental disagreement over outcomes. For now, the dialectic of party-political interests holds supremacy over discussion and agreement of what constitutes the national interest (2009:21).

In simple terms, an election had been stolen from the MDC, in glaring views of everyone, so why they negotiated as if they were the thieves, not the victims, shows how immature their leadership and the MDC are. Even though Mugabe was the person the whole world was vilifying over the breakdown of the country, he still stood by his position, and got the deal he wanted for his party. Some might argue that Mugabe also sacrificed power, but the question is to whom he shared that power with. Not the MDC or maybe the MDC didn't know how to exercise the power Mugabe lost. This power-sharing only found meaning on the text it was written with on the paper, but in actuality, it didn't exist.

I know a lot of people would disagree with me, citing that the country was going through a devastating cholera epidemic, and that things were haywire, economically speaking, and that it was imperative that Tsvangirai had to enter into governance, to stench this breakdown and devastating cholera. The cholera epidemic was being sorted-out with, even at that, little government help, by the donors, so it wasn't the MDC's immediate problem. The economy was the headache of the ZANU-PF, and it had created that, so it was up to the ZANU-PF to figure out solutions to its problems. The MDC should have stayed out, and let the economic problems that the

ZANU-PF didn't know how to solve decide the destiny of the country. It's a difficult stance, but no country, anywhere in the world, has ever been won by playing the nice policemen. We lost over 50 000 people during the independence war, in nearly 2 decades of fighting, to get Ian Smith to negotiate to relinquish power. This situation was even different. There was little bloodshed so Tsvangirai could have ill-afforded to stay out; just selfishly doing that knowing it would solve the problems.

There was not much of a way to go for the ZANU-PF before even ZANU-PF could have given up, and negotiated with little or no power. We were almost there, but due to, the political immaturity of the MDC, they accepted this "stupid deal". They should have said "NO" to SADC, AU, who were pushing them to accept, and allow the ZANU-PF to create its own government without them, just like they have done now post-July 2013 elections.

It might be due to greed for power that the MDC, and especially Tsvangirai, accepted this deal. He had fought for so long, since 1989, in the ZCTU, for power against the same person. I think he was now tired of staying out. Taking into consideration that he had been an insider in the ZANU-PF (party commissar), so he must have longed for the power of home. He knew Mugabe could have created his own government without him. What he didn't understand was that that government had little life. He should have stayed out and see that government bombing or falling down like dominoes.

He fell for the sugared positions that Mugabe was offering, just like Nkomo did in 1987, and Nkomo was swallowed by Mugabe. This time Mugabe didn't want to swallow Tsvangirai, for he knew he would lose a lot of power if he were to swallow the MDC into the ZANU-PF again. And it was going to be obvious it was the same thing he had done to Nkomo, he was doing to Tsvangirai, and so he decided to kill the MDC in this unity government. The MDC also resisted fiercely and insanely to be swallowed, for its life, so instead of the MDC concentrating on important issues, it was stretched in these survival fights in the GNU.

There was even an attempt to kill Tsvangirai, in which he lost his wife. Just losing his wife was enough to destroy Tsvangirai and the MDC, and ever since, Tsvangirai has been a cocoon of his old self. They killed him with that, emotionally. He started making incredible blunders, one after another, the biggest of which is his marriages and love parades. Powerful leaders of the past, like Alexander the Great, Genghis Khan, Shaka Zulu knew well the only way to destroy a very powerful leader was through using women as bait, so they avoided that. It is the siren a lot of leaders wouldn't resist. Bill Clinton, I believe he is one of the greatest leaders of the last half century, was almost brought down by Monica Lewinsky, in the 1990s. The ZANU-PF used that on Tsvangirai. It was obvious the space that his wife used to occupy was difficult for Tsvangirai to deal with, and he dealt with it in a very ugly way, womanising his way into his current marriage. He created a lot, in fact the worse publicity through that.

As Tsvangirai was making his seemingly endless love scandals, his councillors were upping the ante in the councils throughout the country, through corruption of allocating themselves residential and commercial stands, stealing council money, misallocating funding for council purposes, awarding themselves tenders for council projects and works. In regular talks I have had with a friend, of my street, Prosper Mlambo, he always centre on how much corruptive the MDC has been by just focusing on our councillor, who prior to his election into the council, he was an informal small tools trader at the local Zengeza 2 Council Market. But, in less than 5 years in the council, he had a massive residential property, several stands and a fleet of cars etc... I am not saying the ZANU-PF councillors were not doing the same, too. Every Zimbabwean knows, and has always accepted that as the norm with the

ZANU-PF, but for the party they had supported to oust the ZANU-PF from power to stop these corruptive tendencies to just take to this smash and grab mentality of the ZANU-PF was difficult for a lot of people to accept.

The minister responsible for local and urban authorities, Ignatius Chombo, kept a blind eye to this corruption, feeding on it as well, and allowed it to fester, and when it had spread throughout the country's cities, he started making political mileage with the clean-up, or even expositions of these scandals, and the whole ZANU-PF campaign machine, including the public media milked this. In his divorce settlements, a couple or so years ago, Chombo's wife brought it forth in the media that Chombo had nearly 200 properties in Zimbabwe's cities. This can only be through corruption for how could you account for a government minister, who had been in the government for nearly 15 years, could amass such wealth in this little time. It means he was buying in excess of 15 properties every year. Before that he was just a lecturer at the University of Zimbabwe, so all these properties were amassed in 15 years he has served in the government, not to talk of other businesses he owns, farms, etc...

But, for the MDC, they took no other alternatives but to exe most of these councillors found corruptive from both their positions in the council and the MDC. As expounded by Masunungure and Bratton (2011):

> We were told that the top MDC leader is dead set against corruption, which he would root out of the party because his own credibility was at stake. There is some evidence to support this claim since at least two of the MDC ministers (Fedelis Mhashu and Elias Mudzuri) who were rumoured to have taken bribes were demoted in a Cabinet reshuffle in July 2010. So, Tsvangirai took immediate action to suspend, investigate and dismiss local government councillors from MDC when they were

charged with misallocating council houses and other improprieties (p.46).

Some people say it's a mistake he made. That, the MDC should have recalled these councillors from council, but not expunging them out of the party, and allowed them to go through re-claiming, re-adjustment, and re-learning programs, so that they could be reassigned in the future, once they had learned their lessons. ZANU-PF has done that with most of its people, the likes of Dzikamai Mavhaire, Cephas Msipa, Enos Nkala, Fredrick Shava, Jonathan Moyo, Kumbirai Kangai, and Didymus Mutasa etc…, in actual fact, the list is endless with the ZANU-PF.

It makes me go back to the argument I made in, ZIMBABWE: THE BLAME GAME, in the essay, MALEMANIA, that the things that the ANC were accusing Julius Malema of doing, generally of bringing disrepute to the ANC, were even the things that President Jacob Zuma was doing, at a larger scale, with his scandals, but little was being done to bring him to book. I will use the same argument here. The things, or scandals the councillors were being accused of doing, bringing disrepute to the MDC, the MDC president was doing worse than these councillors, with his love and marriage scandals, but nobody had gumption enough in the MDC to stand up to Tsvangirai, and try to discipline him, or even make him go through re-corrective measures or courses. He was the president so he was above any censure. And, it's what we have come to realise about our leaders in Zimbabwe, and Africa at large. They are made to stand above the law, and could do as they wished.

These love scandals and mismanagement or scandals of the councillors were one of the biggest MDC's undoing in the GNU entity. Their limitations were exposed endlessly in the public platforms. This brings me to an important issue, and the question, where were the policemen (women), spokeswomen

(men), publicist, and thinkers of the MDC. These, it seems, went to sleep in the MDC. There was no policing in the MDC of Tsvangirai and the councillors' reckless behaviours. The publicists and spokespersons, like Tsvangirai's spokesperson and aides (he had a full office of these people in the GNU), or the MDC's spokesperson, all left him as he bombed with his scandals. A few of their thinkers were in the GNU government itself and were left with little time to focus on party business, such that they lost on footing the party in the right path.

Bratton and Masunungure (2011:45), also goes further and indict the MDC president and party on this issue,

> But the leaders who could devote their efforts and expertise to this task have been co-opted into the transitional government. For example, the Secretary General (Tendai Biti) of the MDC-T doubles as the Minister of Finance in the GNU and his party deputy is Minister of Economic Planning and Investment Promotion (Tapiwa Mashakada). Moreover, the top ranks of MDC-T are thin with personnel who have any experience at governing. On these grounds alone, the MDC is ill-prepared to complete a regime transition, to take power, or to govern. Moreover, neither MDC party is internally democratic, with top leaders revealing tendencies to ignore party rules, overrule popular decisions.

One of which is when Tsvangirai overruled the MDC's decision to participate in the 2005 senate vote, which brought on the 2005 schism and breakup of the MDC. He is also known to recklessly dismiss dissident voices. Bratton and Masunungure (2011:46) developing their arguments from Chan's (2008) observations go further,

> Indeed, the qualities and depth of Morgan Tsvangirai as a leader have been questioned. A biographer described him

as "a hit-and-miss politician – capable of strokes of genius but also prone to periods of wayward and ineffectual leadership." For example, he has been slow to mediate a growing rivalry inside MDC-T between Tendai Biti, party Secretary General and Ian Makone, secretary to the PM who serves as a major private donor and the party's last Director of Elections. On the other hand, Tsvangirai has shown an even temperament as Prime Minister, along with genuine concern for popular suffering and flashes of statesmanship. And in the treacherous terrain of Zimbabwe's elite politics he has displayed exceptional bravery and citizens have credited him for this and rewarded him with their votes. Despite the best efforts of ZANU-PF to portray otherwise, there is little sign of a serious internal leadership challenge to Tsvangirai.

Although I don't agree with Bratton and Masunungure's last observation, I agree with their general statement above. Threat to Tsvangirai's leadership has festered for some time now. It started in the 2005 breakup that gave birth to the Ncube lead MDC. It also festered badly when he squashed on his left-wing group who didn't want to enter the GNU, who included Tendai Biti, who was vocal against the deal curved. Thus, in this regard, MDC-T is now more factionalised and consumed by internal succession struggles like the ZANU-PF.

It doesn't mean the ZANU-PF peers were not doing the same bungling in the unity government that the MDC-T was doing but there were policemen, publicists, and aides in the ZANU-PF that managed their scandals, so that they couldn't enter the public domain. That's why now the whole country is shell-shocked by the corruption and bloated salaries that ZANU-PF appointed people in the public and parastatals are said to be earning. Why it wasn't exposed during the GNU tells you about how the ZANU-PF manages its dirty. But, in the MDC during the GNU, nobody was there to stop or give advice to Tsvangirai. There were no thinkers to help the MDC to think of their life beyond the GNU entity.

The ZANU-PF had huge and experienced thinkers like Professor Jonathan Moyo, Cephas Msipa, Dzikamai Mavhaire, and many others, who were not in the GNU, but who concentrated on charting the way forward for the ZANU-PF. It is safe to say the MDC doesn't have these in its hierarchy, as I have alluded to before, because of the breakdown of the party after the 2005 schism, in which some went to form the other MDC, like professor Welshman Ncube, the death of professor Mukonoweshuro, Gibson Sibanda, Lovemore Matombo etc... They don't seem to be people who think above themselves in this party, who think on a bigger platform.

All the current crop of leaders in the MDC cares about is about their positions in the party, enriching positions. We might want to rush and blame Tsvangirai that he doesn't think, he is stupid, that he makes a lot of goofs, but even stupid presidents like George Bush managed to win an election, twice at that; and was the president of the USA for 8 years. He had huge thinkers behind him who would give him advice, and choreography his presidency like Dick Chaney, Condoleezza Rice, etc…, so what Tsvangirai needed were people behind him who would do the thinking for him. Yes, I know that wouldn't have ensconced him from making his usual blunders, speech blunders, but those were not big problems, as such. In fact, they made us laugh, a bit. Bush had lots of these, too; but he still managed to carry on. So it seems, the MDC's larger problem, in the meanwhile, is to find thinkers, people who can think outside their boxes.

We got to an election, and the MDC was not even prepared for it because they were no people making the party gear up for this election. If the MDC thought they were not going to be an election, after 5 years of the GNU entity, then its petty thinking on their side. They should have been prepared for it, but all they did was waste time in making the

ZANU-PF to conform to negotiations, as I have argued above.

I will conclude this essay stating that these GNU entities are not right for development of democracy, as witnessed on Zimbabwe and Kenya. Mapuva (2010:250) is of the same thinking, saying,

> GNUs on the African continent have come to represent a short-cut to those who want to cling to power and even promote electoral inconsistency to achieve this objective. As a result, democracy has been dealt a heavy blow by the GNU phenomenon, which appears to have emerged in many countries where rival political parties unite after disputed elections to form an inclusive government in the interim and to implement structural political reforms. However, despite justifications for this form of political arrangement, political scientists have predicted that this formation could herald the demise of democracy on the continent. Of immediate recall would be events in Kenya (December 2008) and in Zimbabwe, which vividly illustrate this emerging trend.

In both countries now, both parties and or persons (Tsvangirai, and Odinga) that had won the election, who were forced to share the government with the losers, have now been defeated, and are now outside government.

Chapter 4

Dairy Extracts from, *IT'S NOT ABOUT ME*

Wednesday, December 22, 2010

.... There was no electricity all morning. They are rationing it, have been rationing it for nearly a decade now, without any solutions. It's even an insult to say they are rationing it, as if it would change very soon and we would have all the electricity we want. This is "normal". You have to make it normal, so that it won't bother you too much. It's the little boys and girls who create ceremony out of this electricity rationing. When it goes out, they would shout in the streets, that, "electricity is gone", and when it comes back they celebrate as if the Zimbabwe National Soccer Team has scored a goal against the Pharaohs, maybe. One would think there has been a game on the go, all along. Why the Egyptians; we have rivalry that goes back to early 1990s, football-wise. So, the electricity was restored at about midday with fanfare in the streets. I could not play music to blot out the noise, all morning, so I couldn't focus on anything. It was as if electricity lights up my mind; to start thinking, feeling, writing.

Wednesday, January 5, 2011

It's debilitating, not only the heat, that music of hopelessness in the air. It permeates the outside shell of things-being-fine propaganda here. The all-around happiness is so farce especially now in January when people start to deal with the real issues; children school fees, post-holiday stress, going back to work, little or no more money. The political machine is in full swing. Yesterday ZANU-PF was doing its usual trickery, of giving the old people things like fertilizers to buy their vote. On the other level, "The Sunday Mail," the government's mouth piece, had a heading, "Elections Maybe Deferred." The contradictions are ZANU-PF power play and elections gymnastics. It's been like that for many years. It's a game. It means the elections are most likely to be held this year if Mugabe has his way. ZANU-PF doesn't even take kindly to the situation obtaining now in the country where-by it is being forced to share power. The situation is too stable for ZANU-PF. They want a bit more chaos to do business deals, not a controlled atmosphere that is there now. I went into Harare city centre today. I have been looking for bookshops that were willing to take in new authors. It was disappointing to hear the only buyer interested saying that they could only take my collection of poetry, Voices from Exile, at a quarter of its actual price. The market is dead to say the least. I couldn't give them the collection on that price. When coming back, and on entering Chitungwiza from Harare, the main road was so broken down, so eaten out, around the ST Mary's CA area. A few men had taken over the maintenance of this road. They were repairing the road using stones and rubble and asking for some coins to passing motorist as payment. You would wonder what the city fathers were doing at their offices in Tilcor road. These men, though, were so hilarious and funny altogether but the sad fact is that nobody thought it was an important thing to repair these roads, something that was in such dire need of repair?

Tuesday, May 3, 2011

I had to release my anger and pent up frustrations on the city council (Zengeza branch) people. I went there to check whether they had sorted our home services account, which I had left with these people in the beginning of the previous month. Apparently they hadn't done anything so I had to wait whilst the guy (a certain Mudzudza) worked out the problem. The problem was because of our metre that was dysfunctional. It had stood for years on the 4911 reading (2006-), but all of a sudden it had started working, a couple or so months or even years, I am not sure. It had had about 80 kilolitres and they hadn't started recording but were still using the estimates, which is an unbelievable 35 kilolitres for a month. How can a single person use that lake of water? 35 kilolitres is too much, but that's what we were being charged for over 5 yrs now. Our metre was like Jesus who rose from the dead, I pointed that out to the city guy as I let rip this guy, but it didn't serve much purpose other than loosening me a bit, and the cutting back of the credit by about 40 dollars.

Thursday, June 30, 2011

Our area is in Zengeza 1. The part of our area covers the following streets, Guyo, Rusero, Mutsi, Svosve and Mubvumira Streets. It is adjacent to Zengeza 2 Shopping Centre. The place has blocks, detached, box houses; houses of two small bedrooms, a dining room, and a kitchen, plus a double functional toilet and bathroom cubicle. At our place I am using two rooms, bedroom and dining room, and another family of 3; father, mother and a little kid are using the other two rooms, the kitchen and another bedroom. We share the small toilet-cum-bathroom place. Some households can count up to 15 people on the same small house. In our street there are 45 households, crammed on an area that covers 35 metres by maybe 110 metres; a football pitch is bigger than our street. Our home is about 13 metres by 6 metres. There are over 400 people in our street, so I think you get an idea of how crammed up it is. That applies to the other streets that make up our area, and ultimately the biggest part of the entire city, Chitungwiza. When I came back from South Africa I thought I was going to see the city halved of its massive populations due to the migrations that had happened over the years, but it seems, there are more people than, say, over 5 years ago. I discovered the same thing with my Church, my old church which has swelled considerably since the time I left. I am saying this considering, like I have alluded above, there is a massive number of the country's population now staying outside the country. Some parts of Johannesburg are predominantly Shona speaking areas. One would almost think they won't be a lot of people still left in the country considering also the scourge of HIV/AIDS that devastated the country for the last 2 decades, but no, people are marrying, having babies as if nothing is the matter, thereby overpopulating an already overpopulated, and poor country. Pretty very few people go to work in Chitungwiza so it's an informal life that the people lead here. The young people are desponded. I sometimes refer to the place, Chitungwiza, or Zimbabwe, as a hospital of hopeless people. It definitely is. So, maybe marrying, or having sex, mostly unprotected and having unplanned pregnancies and kids is their drug they take to deal with the despondency, thereby populating the place and negatively impacting on their despondency state. I know they want to have hope but there is nowhere to begin with for the lot of them so they are like people in a prison serving a lifetime prison sentence. They have to pay up for the crimes they never really committed, in an open prison, but still imprisoned anyway. By the lack of something to do to vault themselves out of these ghettos or the country, and it's like getting into such a hell whereby the devil is committed to burning you slowly, on a small fire, such that it takes you a long, a terribly long, long time to die, or even, to not even feel anything in this hell. Sometimes, I am feeling like that these days, hopeless; asking myself constantly whether I am going to finally get out of this hell, as well.

Monday, August 22, 2011

It's Monday morning after an interesting week. In this week we witnessed the death of Solomon Mujuru, a former commander of the Defence Forces, during the liberation war and after. He was burned to beyond recognition at his farm in the Beatrice area, south of Harare, along Masvingo highway, about 60 km from Harare. Theories have been abounding as to the cause of the fire, especially that he could have been burned, or killed in politically motivated violence. The much talked about camps in the ZANU-PF party draws from two camps. One led by Solomon Mujuru and another led by Emerson Mnangagwa (the present Defence minister), who is a powerful politician in Zimbabwe's political field, as well. Mugabe is always playing around these two camps, thus these are made into squabbling little children's groups by Mugabe, and it stays Mugabe in power in the ZANU-PF and Zimbabwe. That's how he has been playing his games, the old wiser. The Mujuru camp includes the wife of Mujuru, who is the vice president and most of Mashonaland provinces' big political gurus. That's why, maybe, Sydney Sekeramayi (the Security minister and the favoured successor to Mugabe, according to other pundits) was crying, was choking with emotions on the first day after Mujuru's death, even though Mai Mujuru (Joyce Mujuru) was not showing any emotions at all, I suppose maybe she was trying to be stately in the funeral. She wasn't even on leave, didn't take leave of duty to mourn her husband. I thought, in actual fact, I felt that Mai Mujuru was full of anger and wrath, at the ZANU-PF, or maybe at her husband or the killers. It's understandable. Emotions and feelings are a wild creature. There is no one way in which they have to be shown. Maybe, after the anger, she will show a bit of emotion and vulnerability. I thought even some of the anger was directed at the president. I would understand that: Mugabe should know what's happening. She made an ugly face or angry face at the president when the president was offering his condolences. I felt he was laughing, gloating with glee in his take of the situation as he said, in that iconic tone of his when making fun and insulting political opponents, that he has never seen anyone getting burned to that extent; beyond recognition, in a fire. The way he was saying it was callous, and unfeeling, as if he was happy he had one devil less to deal with now. Maybe Mai Mujuru felt exposed; felt she was now in the open, without anyone to defend her from the ZANU-PF political power play and machinations. Even though there has been speculation, for years, that the two, the Mujurus were since separated, I feel it was still a bitter loss for Mai Mujuru. Solomon Mujuru has always protected Mai Mujuru, knowing full well it would bode well for the two of them, if they worked together as a team, and for their children. They are said to be one of the wealthiest family in the country, through this working together. Even Mugabe is said to have been afraid of "The General" as Solomon Mujuru was referred to. There was a moment, some years ago; at around the 2008 elections when Mujuru was linked to the Simba Makoni's project (later Mavambo party). They even went together, with Simba, to confront and sell the Simba Makoni idea to Mugabe, asking the old man to simply step down from ZANU-PF and allow Makoni to be the election face for the ZANU-PF party. Both were told to go to hell by the old man. Mujuru's confrontation with the old man, it was said by the old man himself, didn't last for more than 5 minutes. There was speculation at that time that the old boy threatened to strip Mai Mujuru of the vice presidency in the ZANU-PF, and Solomon, of all the wealth he had accumulated and of any respect (burial at the heroes acre is one of the issues trumped , as well). So really they were not great friends, Mujuru and Mugabe. He wasn't best buddies with Mnangagwa either. It took Mnangagwa over 2 days to pay his condolences to the vice president. After, I should think when Mujuru

35

the wife, had come out squashing the rumour mills, saying as to the politically motivated killings charge, that the people, and the Mujurus themselves had accepted the death as God's design. And that everyone else should accept it as that. That, there is no witch-hunt, and then, Mnangagwa came out from hiding and paid his condolences and instantly took over as the leader of the army in giving the respect deservedly to Mujuru. Then his condolence messages instantly became the most aired on the television, and it was the longest convoluted mourning speech I have ever heard, and it was trumped up by the propaganda television station ZTV. It was mostly a talk about ZANU-PF and himself, not about the deceased, as if he was the one dead. Maybe, he knows he is now dead. He is no longer a rival to anyone, really. The camp can still be there, the Mujuru camp but it would have no recognisable head now, so it would be difficult to fight something that doesn't have a head. Joyce Mujuru will be the leader of this camp and she is a woman. It's not easy to fight against a woman. You are easily exposed out on the open. Mujuru's wife isn't one who would like to openly play to this camp thing, for she knows she is the next in line, after Mugabe, as long as she behaves well towards Mugabe. Mugabe will always protect her interests so why bother with the dirty people like Mnangagwa. The other funny aspect of the funeral is that instead of Mugabe giving Mujuru some time to attend the funeral of her dead husband, he refused her the most descent thing, by abandoning her with country as the acting president whilst this naked emperor gallivanted to Angola for their SADC talkathon summit. I don't know what John Nkomo was doing (there is even speculation that he is very ill, though), for he should have been left presiding, or Mugabe should have sent someone else to SADC (Mnangagwa, maybe), or appoint someone else to act on his capacity as the president, not Mujuru who was dealing with her loss. Even Tsvangirai wasn't given the mandate to chair the cabinet, reneging on the GNU provisions that stated that the prime minister would chair the cabinet in the president's absence. It's obvious that Mugabe doesn't trust anyone else other than those who really surround him (Mujuru and Nkomo), or that he is plain cruel. I think it goes both ways, the answer does. Even Ian Khama (Botswana president) didn't attend the SADC meeting but instead sent his deputy. He was on a state visit in West

Africa region for bilateral talks, so it meant someone else, not the president himself, was acting in Botswana in the absence of the two in Botswana. Why not in Zimbabwe?

****

On Friday morning I tried to listen, in fact, I listened to 7 "O" clock news; Good Morning Zimbabwe News. It took over 36 minutes of the 60 minutes, the presenter, Tracy Sibanda, talking about Mujuru. And, I thought that's the last of it, no, it wasn't. It seems everyone was jostling to have their faces and voices be heard and be seen on the television. Even the provincial nobodies, from all over the country, did a great job. But, it's Mnangagwa who had taken the centre stage. Business news was also about Mujuru and his business exploits. Sports news was also about Mujuru and his sporting exploits. I don't know what sport this guy did, or was involved in, to deserve this feature, other than maybe the Army team Black Rhinos which he might have been involved in, in its formation days. Apparently, it was when he was the general of Zimbabwe's army when Rhinos football club was formed (83-85), and had its glory days. So Mujuru featured for the allotted 60 minutes of the entire news programme. This is the first time, in a long haul, that Mugabe news or news about Mugabe took the back seat, and it was refreshing, just for that. The last time I can remember was when Simon Muzenda, that larger-than-life character died when Mugabe news was overshadowed. So, this larger-than-life general had overshadowed Mugabe, especially in his death. Even what was discussed at SADC, and it was about Zimbabwe's political situation, wasn't as important to the ZTV, even though there were important issues discussed there. Is Mujuru more important than Zimbabwe itself? And yes, the talks on Zimbabwe are still continuing, still talking about talks, I suppose.

****

Late on Friday (20 August) I had one of those marathon talks with a certain guy about Zimbabwe's problems. I have often talked to this friend about such issues before. It goes way back, but here it was about where the country was heading towards. This friend supports the other faction of the MDC, the Mutambara faction, or more appropriately now, the Ncube faction. Mutambara was kicked out by Ncube so it seems to be in a limbo, this MDC, and Mutambara is in a limbo, as well. He seems to be going the ZANU-PF way. He is courting the ZANU-PF party, is always toeing to the ZANU-PF line on the Zimbabwean issue. I have always thought the likes of Mutambara and Makoni are not genuine opposition members, are ZANU-PF's game making ideas, so also to a certain extent, Welshman Ncube. Mugabe even doesn't waste his time criticising these, but Morgan Tsvangirai and Tendai Biti of the main MDC party, whom he is always trashing, even though they are now partners in this GNU monster. I tried to feel, through this friend, what this other MDC is now all about since Ncube took over. Has its lines changed to real opposition politics? Last election it sold out on Zimbabwe's electorate by backing Simba Makoni rather than Morgan Tsvangirai who had real chances of upstaging Mugabe and defrauded the entire nation of victory against Mugabe. The 8 percentage that Makoni got should have helped Tsvangirai secure the required 51 percentage to form a government, but these guys were stupid and petulant. It still seems a muddy pool to me. You can't even figure out what they stand for, other than benefiting through donor funding or a possible merger with the larger MDC. It seems they are even prepared again to take away the votes from the larger MDC, Tsvangirai's MDC, as long as they are going to get money for funding from donors for such endeavour. They are pretty-prepared to up the ante in obtaining this situation so they would remain relevant. He was even saying he foresaw another power-sharing arrangement after the elections. This is what I really don't want to see happening to us again.

****

Thursday, September 22, 2011

It is like a hospital of the hopeless: Life in Zimbabwe is like that. It's obvious when you have a closer look at the people. In my street, I was

38

*surprised to hear that they were over 3 guys who went bonkers, some tried
to kill themselves, some tried to kill others. There are several girls who are
staying home, unmarried, some with their own children, after failing to get
married. Lots of them are staying with men who haven't paid lobola, some
of the men don't have the wherewithal. And the girls have resorted to
prostitution, and a lot of men are thieves, vagabonds. Mothers now choose
who they want their children to be married to. It is always about money.
The girls have lots and lots of boyfriends, some to carter for their financial
needs, some as prospective husbands. There are no jobs being created, save
only in the civil service, so most of the brightest minds are ending up being
teachers and nurses, police and army people. Going to the university seems
a waste of time because you won't get employed after finishing your 4 year
degree. There are several I know in my street who are sitting on their
university degrees, or have now started on another path, different from the
one they had studied. There is simply no work. Those who have been in the
workplace have been in the same position for over 5 years. My former
manager at AMTEC Motors, for 4 years there, is still on the same
position, for 8 years now. There are no better prospects for the lot so they
are staying put. The good thing is the economy has stabilized due to the use
of the United States dollar, such that it isn't that unpredictable, like 3
years ago, but it's very painful, all the same. It's a slow, slow painful, drip,
drip, dying or life. The prospect of or the hope that someday it will change
is all that drives people to keep going. But, the truth is, it would take a
lifetime to get things right again. There is still a lot of work that needs to
be put into, to change the course of things here and the first stop is the
political situation, and it's a big, big ask. Those who left the country do
not want to return, because, really, there is nothing to return home for.*

Chapter 5

SADC, AU, International Community's Shortcomings

Starting way back after the 2002 presidential election when SADC started dibbling in Zimbabwe democratisation processes, all through the years until the hotly disdained June 2008 poll, the belief was it was the SADC that had to solve Zimbabwe's problems. There is a time when the likes of Olusegan Obasanjo, Kofi Annan, and George Bush etc..., tried to intervene in the negotiations and the expulsion of Zimbabwe from the commonwealth, but the South African presidency, especially Thabo Mbeki, felt the solution had to be mediated by the SADC, with South African mediation. He even told George Bush "hands off" Zimbabwe, criticising the Western nations when they tried to have the issue discussed at the United Nations Security Council, and South Africa galvanised China and Russia to vote against imposition of sanctions on Zimbabwe. It got to a point when the world over accepted that it's the SADC that had to solve Zimbabwe's problems.

Though, I believe the SADC had better understanding of the issues to deal with Zimbabwe and had to be on the fore front, but we needed the issue to be solved on a broader level, with the direct involvement of the AU, and the UN, such that there was going to be better generation of ideas, management, monitoring and implementation of the problems. For the entire world to accept the SADC had to solve Zimbabwe's problems was an oversight, especially on the UN that has more authority over nations.

This has resulted in a lot of problems to the negotiations, implementation, and post-implementation process. Bratton and Masunungure (2011:34) posit,

> The fundamental problem with the transitional government is that power is not shared, but divided. ZANU-PF and MDC-T exercise power separately within largely exclusive, and often competing, zones of authority. Moreover the distribution of power is unequal, with the balance tilted in favour of old guard elements from the previous regime. Thanks to its intransigent stance during power-sharing talks, ZANU-PF managed to retain exclusive control over the coercive instruments of state, including the security, intelligence, and judicial services, as well as the politically strategic ministries responsible for land, agriculture, and local government. MDC was unsuccessful in a bid to obtain a Deputy Minister post in the Ministry of Defence, instead accepting that ZANU-PF would be denied a similar position in the Ministry of Finance. And, under intense pressure on an issue that threatened to derail the entire settlement, MDC was forced by the South African negotiators to accept co-leadership with ZANU-PF of the Ministry of Home Affairs, which controls the police. Moreover, a patronage culture endures.

The global political agreements were not fulfilled before the July 2013 elections. What the whole process managed to achieve was the creation of a constitution. The other issues that were to be addressed like ZEC reforms, Security sector reforms, media reforms, electoral laws reforms, the flattening of the playing ground with equal sharing of other important government posts in the GNU, posts like the director generals, permanent secretaries, governorships, ambassadors were not implemented. It begs a huge question why the AU observer mission, headed by Olusegan Obasanjo declared the elections as free and fair. The question begs; can it be possible for an observer to declare an election as fair when the reforms that had to be sorted-out before an election were not done before the election. How could someone say the election was fair, let alone credible? It's easier to say there were no harassments, killings, or any other abuses you could think of, two weeks before the election and during the election time, so the elections had to be free and fair. But, if all the issues that had to be implemented, especially the contentious issue of security sector reforms were not addressed, it surely caused some people to question the whole process, let alone to vote in these elections. How could one go and cast his or her vote knowing that a win for the opposition might result in disturbances and militarisation of the country by the security establishment, which still had the same leaders who still refused to acknowledge the opposition, who had also fermented the post-2008 election militarisation and violence in the country.

The problem is, and has always been with Zimbabwe; it's the same people who have been policemen, culprits, and final judges who are made to decide the destiny of the country. Chitiyo (2009: 20) observes that the problem with the GNU negotiated and accepted was on *Presidential and Prime Ministerial Powers*,

> The Zimbabwean Constitution stipulates that the president has the right to appoint or dismiss ministers. The GPA stipulates that the president has to consult with the prime minister before appointing or removing cabinet members. (The MDC dispute this clause saying that in the original GPA agreement, the president needs the assent of the prime minister before making this executive decision).

Chitiyo was referring to the old constitution that was in use concurrently with the GPA stipulations before the new constitution was created and adopted to become legal tender.

As an example of how this law was interpreted and caused disagreements between the two parties in the government, Chitiyo argues,

> …the president's decision to remove control of the ICT Ministry from Nelson Chamisa. Nevertheless, the continued farm invasions, and the ongoing harassment of MDC personnel, have raised doubts as to whether the prime minister is willing to challenge the president on matters of principle or substance (2009:20).

The problem was he couldn't challenge Mugabe much because Mugabe was using the old constitution of the country in making these decisions that gave him the powers, which the SADC negotiators failed to share it out in the GPA stipulations. His prime minister's position was powerless in the GPA.

The other problem with the GNU was there has not been any outside monitoring of the entire programme, so that what had been agreed to could really be implemented. And, in their paper on, *SADC's Role in Zimbabwe*, Dzinesa and Zambara (undated: 65) called it, "The Fallacy of Self-Monitoring", saying

There have been some serious challenges with the implementation of the GPA. The MDC has persistently raised concerns about the appointment of provincial governors, diplomats, senior public servants, the Attorney General Johannes Tomana and the Reserve Bank Governor Gideon Gono, as well as the arrest of some of its Members of Parliament. ZANU-PF, for its part, has complained about the continuation of sanctions imposed on many of its senior figures, the reported establishment of parallel government structures by Prime Minister Tsvangirai's office and the generally anti-ZANU-PF radio broadcasts that are still being beamed into Zimbabwe from abroad. These issues could, and should, have been monitored and resolved. But there was no independent body to do it. Arguably, the main mistake SADC made was that it did not establish impartial structures to effectively monitor and evaluate the implementation of the GPA, which it had so painstakingly helped to negotiate. Instead, a Joint Monitoring and Implementation Committee (JOMIC), comprising members of the three coalition partners, was established to ensure the parties' compliance with the GPA. But JOMIC has been a toothless bulldog.

They were commenting on the SADC's belief that Zimbabwe had to solve its own problems and monitor the process on their own, with little supervision from the SADC.

Even the cabinet that came out from this type of negotiation was bloated. In the first days of the negotiations, the idea was to create a small cabinet that would cut on the government bill. Considering that we were going through unprecedented economic, social and political problems, this was called for, but they ended up bloating it altogether, to take into account all their major players and constituencies in their parties, and as well giving each other the opportunity to enrichment. Bratton and Masunungure (2011:34) observe:

> The Global Political Agreement called for a six-person executive (a president and prime minister, each with two deputies) and a large cabinet of 31 ministers and 16 deputy ministers. Yet the accord was violated at birth when ZANU-PF and the two MDC's colluded to appoint 41 ministers and 19 deputies, the largest and most expensive cabinet in Zimbabwe's history. The expansion of official posts to accommodate political allies suggests that both sides were willing expediently to sacrifice the careful management of scarce public resources in order to distribute political spoils. And some MDC cadres may well regard a government position as an opportunity to gain access to assets and rents previously enjoyed by ZANU-PF,

as reflected in demands for state-of-the-art vehicles and other perks by MPs across the three parties.

Dzinesa and Zambara (undated: 65) note JOMIC problems:

> This JOMIC was flawed from the start because it made the three political parties both the players and the referees, leaving full implementation of the GPA vulnerable to non-compliance by any of the parties since there was no effective external supervision by SADC. Perhaps the regional body deliberately intended not to be seen as infringing on Zimbabwe's sovereignty in a continent where sovereignty is the last line of defence, and in a region in which elite political camaraderie still holds sway. Whatever the reason, relying on self-monitoring by the parties to the GPA meant that SADC was unable to assert its authority over the implementation of the agreement. This has been a determining factor in the parties, especially ZANU-PF's, non-compliance with the GPA, which has on numerous occasions threatened to derail the entire transitional arrangement. External involvement and pressure was further limited in the Zimbabwean context by ZANU-PF's clarion call against imperialism, neo-colonialism and non-interference in the affairs of a sovereign state.

This resulted in the constitution process gobbling most of the negotiations, running behind schedule and it provided arguably the clearest example of SADC's ineffective intervention post the inauguration of the GNU. This constitution making program that should have taken 18 months, according to the GPA stipulation, took all the 5 years of the GNU life. SADC didn't have monitors to observe this process, neither any other reforms that had to be made, thus nothing else was done. Dzinesa and Zambara (undated: 65) go on and give an example of how we could have learned lessons from the Kenyan example saying,

> Lessons could have been learned from Kenya, where the process was completely different. Following the post-election violence in 2007, mediation by an AU Panel of Eminent African Personalities chaired by former United Nations Secretary General Kofi Annan also led to the establishment of a coalition government as a means to institute comprehensive political reforms. But, crucially, civil society was tasked with monitoring the unity government. Social Consulting, a non-governmental organisation with expertise in governance and social development, was contracted to independently monitor the implementation of the Kenya Peace Accord and provide regular reports to the High Level Panel of Prominent Persons on any achievements as well as any challenges or issues that needed to be addressed.

And this is what the organization; Social Consulting Group had to say as quoted in Dzinesa and Zambara (undated: 65):

> By their very nature coalitions are politically fragile. They comprise different and dynamic political entities that work jointly while preserving their individual identities. It is difficult, therefore, for coalition partners to monitor or track their progress on their own because individual interests may influence how they see and interpret this progress. Therefore, in order to keep focused on the goal of the National Accord, there is a need to regularly track or monitor progress made in implementing action points on each agenda item. An external and independent assessment is important in showing progress or lack of it in implementation of each agenda item. This is also critical in

47

identifying and providing feedback on progress, challenges and gaps in implementation.

Bratton and Masunungure (2011:34-35) agree,

But, so far, in Zimbabwe (in contrast to the dynamics of power sharing in Kenya), contestation between rival elites is far more common than collusion. The GPA signatories rarely work well together. Indeed, Mugabe treats Tsvangirai with open contempt. For example, he has systematically prevented the PM from chairing the Cabinet in the President's absence, despite a GPA provision codifying this understanding. And, in practice, the Council of Ministers – which the PM does chair – has been side-lined from a central role in policy debate and is treated as a subcommittee of Cabinet. Nagging disputes over "outstanding issues" of GPA implementation have led MDC Ministers to boycott Cabinet meetings, appeal for the intervention of SADC negotiators, and, in October 2009, to temporarily suspend participation in the coalition government.

Masunungure and Bratton go further:

The sticking points are manifold. First, the president makes all the top appointments. Despite promising to "consult and agree," President Mugabe unilaterally reappointed Gideon Gono as RBZ Governor and Johannes Tomana – responsible for arresting and prosecuting MDC leaders – as Attorney General. After months of wrangling, Tsvangirai announced that permanent secretaries would be allocated proportionally between parties, as would provincial governors (of which MDC-T would get 5, ZANU-PF four, and MDC-M one). But it transpired that presidential authority had secretly been used to reappoint all existing secretaries and that no date had been set to swear in new provincial governors. Then, in October 2010, Mugabe unilaterally reappointed the old ZANU-PF governors without, as required by the GPA, consulting the Prime Minister, prompting yet another walkout from Cabinet by Tsvangirai and charges that the country had entered a constitutional crisis. A generous interpretation of these events was that Mugabe was unable to sell an even-handed division of positions to his own party; a more cynical view is that he acted in bad faith throughout (2011: 35).

The monitoring of the implementation process should have been the job of SADC directorate in Botswana, which couldn't undertake this because of shortage of manpower and finance. Alas the SADC created, later in 2010, a body that should have been monitoring all that, but for a body to be implemented and be expected to cover up on work not done before it came into existence and, do all that work was impossible to expect.

The mediation unit in the SADC Organ on Politics would have the mandate to deal with conflicts within and among member states. I quote Dzinesa and Zambara on the reasons of creating this organ,

This stems from a growing recognition that mediation has been a 'gaping hole' in the regional body's effort to prevent the outbreak of violence between opposing parties. The envisaged mediation structures should be created as part of a comprehensive regional policy and strategy for preventive diplomacy. This is important since experience the world over has demonstrated that preventive diplomacy tools — such as conflict prevention, mediation, good offices, fact-finding missions, negotiation, special envoys, informal consultations, peace building and targeted development activities — can be more useful and cost-effective, as well as being less risky, than military activity in delivering desired peace dividends (undated: 66).

For some, this mediation was now largely viewed as a bilateral issue between South Africa and Zimbabwe, more so when one considers that Jacob Zuma and his team all come from the same political party – the African National Congress – a close ally of ZANU-PF. It was inconceivable to think that they were going to be fair mediation.

These close ally parties (original ANC party splinters; ANC, FRELIMO, SWAPO, UNIP, ZANU-PF, Chama Cha Mapinduzi party) every other year, get together for their mini-congress of some sort, where they discuss issues pertinent to their grouping, one of which has been the belief that these parties feel the western world has been targeting them, and removing them from power, through the financing of the opposition against their rule. It's not possible for me to accept the fact that the ANC would (through its presidency) allow for and force fair play in the negotiations when they know that if they don't protect the ZANU-PF, someday, it would be them on the barrel in South Africa, fighting for their life. Who would protect them if they don't protect their ally now?

Southern Africa has established a normative framework for the conduct of credible and peaceful democratic elections, including the SADC Parliamentary Forum Norms and Standards (2001), the Electoral Institute of Southern Africa/Electoral Commissions' Forum (2003) and the SADC Principles and Guidelines Governing Democratic Elections (2004). These regional guidelines commit SADC member states to follow agreed best election practices. However, the guidelines call for the resolution of election related disputes – like those in Lesotho in 2007 and Zimbabwe – in accordance with their own national laws. This means that SADC is hamstrung in this crucial area since it can only encourage member states to adhere to the SADC principles. It cannot enforce their compliance.

The other problems of the negotiations, implementation, and monitoring of the deal was it was limited to only three political parties and excluded important players like civic organisations. An important organisation like National Consultative Assembly (NCA) that has been focused on the fight toward creating a people driven constitution for the past 2 decades should have been included, especially in the constitution making programme. Other organisations that deserved to be included are labour groups, smaller political parties, NGOs, pressure groups, local area groups, but this exclusivity that the negotiations, implementation and monitoring were smacked of is like the usual fodder from the ZANU-PF rule over the years. We needed participatory democracy.

The other problem was whatever result that came out from the GNU was a political settlement. Even the constitution making programme became a political settlement, whereby when they were disagreements they were settled by just three people, Mugabe, Tsvangirai, and Mutambara, not even consensus from their parties. The three acted throughout the negotiations, implementation and monitoring as if they owned Zimbabwe, and on what pretext is the question. It's them who had the final say on everything, and it's even erroneous to say we got a people driven constitution.

The GNU did not recognize the needs of specific people or victims, like refugees and internally displaced people, let alone those externally displaced, who were completely ignored by both players. Even the body created to deal with this, on National Healing and Reconciliation, was stillborn. Dzinesa and Zambara conclude (undated: 67),

Leaving political parties, who had been at each other's throats for years, to implement the GPA on their own and monitor themselves through JOMIC was probably SADC's most serious misjudgement to date.

South Africa placed itself between a hard place and a rock. On the one hand the country didn't want to be seen as assuming a hegemonic role in the region, yet on the other hand, Zimbabwe was not going to be where it is today without South Africa's leaders, Mbeki, Motlanthe, and Zuma. Somehow whatever happened in Zimbabwe, good or bad, South Africa created or precipitated it, by its sole involvement in this issue. In their paper, THE ANATOMY OF POLITICAL PREDATION, Bratton and Masunungure posit that,

> Political settlements that are externally driven by international actors, hastily negotiated under pressure of time, and reluctantly accepted by the principal parties are unlikely to prove durable or legitimate. Such pacts may quell violence in the short run but they are unlikely to resolve the root causes of political conflict over the long term. One lesson of the Global Political Agreement of 2008 in Zimbabwe is that power-sharing agreements imposed from above by international third parties upon unwilling domestic partners are destined for deadlock, even stalemate (2011:49).

The other problem was the GNU was not made into a binding agreement by the negotiators. Any party to the agreement had every right to get out of the agreement any time it thought or felt its interests were not being fully met. This meant that focus was on what these parties wanted, or were their interests, not the whole country. In case of any party leaving the GNU permanently, the whole agreement would have become null and void, and thus we would have reversed back to what was obtaining before the agreements, with the ZANU-PF in governance. There was not even a clause stipulating that in the case of the GNU's failure, fresh election had to be called with as little time as possible. So, it meant throughout the GNU the ZANU-PF were in the driver's seat. They could frustrate the other players knowing that if these were to leave the agreement, then the ZANU-PF would continue ruling until the end of 5 years. This was another short-sightedness of the agreements that were made from the outside, by the mediation of one person or body.

I would have wanted a situation whereby there were points where the monitoring had to be effected throughout the GNU, whereby specific issues that had to be dealt with were checked whether they had been implemented according to the agreements, and corrective measures put into place in set time periods. Knowing that the Zimbabwean situation is different from the Kenyan situation, the monitors in Zimbabwe's case needed to have been at the level of the UN. The UN accrues a lot of respect and had the power to push through the implementation, than would SADC or local monitoring of the Kenyan case could have achieved. The parties in the GNU needed both a stick and a carrot, and the only stick that could have been effective, in making them follow through with the implementation should have been the UN, which had power to impose sanctions if it found any of the parties scuppering progress toward the implementation of the GNU deal.

The other shortcoming was the international community went to sleep. Pressure on the GNU players was withdrawn by these international players, such that these GNU players worked on their own paces. Embassies, the USA, UK, and EU, which used to make a lot of noise, and applied pressure on the government, stopped putting pressure. The EU even removed most of the members of the ZANU-PF party and companies that had been on targeted sanction lists from the lists. I think, pretty-much everyone went to sleep, thinking and believing the SADC line that these players to the GNU were going to achieve on their promises. Thus, due to this, the GNU failed to achieve on its targets, and we got to an election with very little progress on implementation of the agreements.

Chapter 6

Tuesdays

"Auntie, please Auntie, come back into the kitchen...there is this sound...I am so afraid."

"What sound, Trish?"

"The sound of someone whistling, somewhere at the sink."

"Who could whilst by the sink, Trish?"

"And, he is gloating, guzzling, and gurgling things by his throat."

"What is it, are you crazy, Trish?"

Her auntie comes out of the bedroom, where she was resting, after a very eventful day looking for water, fetching it a kilometre away from their home. When she got to the kitchen she couldn't help laughing, bowling down in laughter. Her body was painful from the work, but she couldn't help laughing. As if by cue the water tape started laughing, too. Trish couldn't understand why that someone who was by the tapes had taken to laughing, like her auntie. She watched her auntie bedazzled by this spectacle...and the water started trickling through the tapes. She joined her auntie, laughing at herself. She was all along afraid of water, coming into the tapes. She hadn't heard that sound, for a couple of years or so, as their tapes had dried out.

It is Tuesday- it is becoming the focus of the week, every week, for about 6 months now. Rhayi was born on a Tuesday, too, but Tuesday now, is when he expects water to come back into the tapes, and any other days; the tapes would create a blank sloshing sound when he opens them. It reminded Rhayi of this story his sister told him, of his niece, Trish. And, there were also many thick jokes made of this situation. Some people said the little kids of the same suburb her sister stayed in had to cry when they saw water trickling into the tapes, not knowing what it was. This place's kids, two or three year olds, hadn't seen water coming out from their tapes, all their little lives, so they were afraid of this occurrence. He had laughed at the jokes, too. But for him, Tuesday is also the day the bins are carted off to the dumping grounds. The two, water coming into the tapes and the carting off of bins, are the only important things the council still do nowadays. He knows it was the two, failure of doing the two well, and it's almost five years ago, that he almost died from cholera. He knows his life, and many other people's lives in this city, hangs on the balance of what happens on these Tuesdays now.

It always starts in the late afternoon of this day...the sloshing, whistling, frothing sounds of the tapes as the water starts flowing...so slowly trickling into the pipes. He personally hates this day, a day shouldn't be this important, he thinks. Also, where he stays, in the back rooms of this property, Rhayi doesn't have an inside tape, so he waits until the water starts flowing through the shower's tape, which would happen at around midnight. Most of these Tuesdays, Rhayi has been having sleepless rough nights. He would set the alarm clock at 12 midnight, and go to sleep at around 8, but sleep won't really come. He doesn't want to miss the alarm, so he generally drifts into sleep, and out of it, for the next 4 hours. There is also noise all around his suburb; his neighbours' shaking cans, gallons, plastic jugs, sometimes hitting them against the sink's basin as they fill these containers with water. Some of his neighbours would be talking to each other, to make it easy, to wait out the night, storing this water into their containers. It is a ritual- like Sunday is a day one would associate with well-dressed people, off to or from the church.

So sleep, he won't on Tuesdays. When the alarm goes off at 12 he has to get out of bed, and start storing the water to use throughout the week. He has two twenty litres plastic buckets, two twenty-five litres plastic containers, 20 plus plastics 2 litres gallons, that he has kept after expending the cooking oil, sour milk or drinks they had contained, in the first place. Rhayi also has a very large dish that would take about 80 litres of water. He has to fill all these containers, water the garden, do plates and dishes, and even washing his clothing. It would be about 4 or 5, or even 7 in the morning, when he is through all this, and thus the Wednesdays are always difficult for him.

He can't concentrate when he is feeling sleepy, so he spends most of these Wednesdays fooling around, or sleeping off this sleep-induced redundancy. Rhayi hates these Tuesdays and Wednesdays, but he has no other alternatives. He can't drink water from the wells that are all over the city. There is too much dirty or sewage flowing around the city for this water to be safe for consumption. Cholera is not a far off memory for him. But, there is something to admire about Wednesdays. It's the only day when he doesn't find a lot of people, all over the neighbourhood, carrying water containers, looking for water, hunting for it. All the other days, there are always a lot of people, in the streets, hunting for this commodity, carrying it off from the wells to their homes.

Sometimes electricity goes out too, but it's usually for some hours. Rationing of electricity has been the catch phrase thing for over a decade now, but at least, it goes for some few hours in a day. But it gets difficult to work through things when electricity is out, as well. There is no music and the place becomes so ugly. It's an ugly place. It has always been music that makes it better. Food would be cold, paraffin is expensive, and so is the wood...it's easier to just eat it cold. At least with water, he knows, he can store some enough to get him through the week.

He can't store electricity in a plastic jug. He learned, a long time ago, electricity is a devastating beast that can't easily be tamed. His old mate, back when he was still at school, tried to do so. He tried to contain it in a radio battery. He climbed the pole, where the lines run through the bushes. He had two wires with him, so he reached the electricity lines unnoticed. He tried to connect those two wires to the electricity line, as well; to the battery he was carrying with him. He was burned into some kind of whiteness. He still carries the burned white skin on him, even today.

But, for Rhayi, this water situation is now a ritual, but he knows it's not a normal situation. He now structures his day around Tuesdays, as if it was a Sabbath day when water filters, or trickles through, like manna from some kind of heaven, into the tapes. And then, another Tuesday, things changed, for the worse. The Tuesday came... and there was no water in the tapes, not even the sloshing, whistling, frothing sound.

On this night he puts his alarm on for twelve, and it chimes, so he wakes up and checks the tapes- there is nothing. He tells himself, maybe at three, so he sets it at three. He checks at three, and there is no water. He knows it is going to be a very difficult week. He goes back to sleep again, and when he wakes up, it is about 8 O'clock, and still there is no water. It's now a Wednesday.

The panic buttons have been pressed, for a lot of the people. People are all over the city, with an assortment of jugs, hunting for water. A local businesswoman who has a Well, who would usually charge 20 cents per container, has now moved to 33 cents, by the end of this Wednesday. The queues have returned. It reminds him of year 2008 when they used to make long queues for pretty-much everything, anything really. Still on this Wednesday, he puts the alarm for 12 and 3, and there is still no water. Thursday morning, it is the talk of the whole city. Before people could even say good morning to each other, the first point of talk is, *"Uri kubuda kupi?"* And someone would answer,

"Nowhere."

"So, where could we get some?" And the answer is usually,

"At Mai Jetty's Well."

"How much is it now?"

"It is now 50 cents for a container." Inwardly he says, to himself, "No, no, I am not going to pay that much for water."

Is the UN aware of this? Water is supposed to be a basic commodity, a basic right, isn't it? He has stopped doing dishes when it didn't return back on Tuesday, so as to preserve on the little he still has. He knows he can stay put on for 2 more days. People are all over, looking for this commodity, selling it, talking about it. It has become the latest street selling adventure for small business people. This old man, maybe he is not that old, raggedly pushes his pushcart full of twenty litres cans of water through the street, shouting in a very high voice, saying, "Water", "Water", "Dollar for two." It's obvious he has found this new trade line. A local despondent man of the street is now charging 20 cents per trip, to carry water jugs, from Mai Jetty's Well. He has anticipated well, on how to make a few bucks for himself and his family.

On Friday morning- it is still a huge scare. There is no water in the tapes. When he is talking to other panicking people he exudes confidence, saying he is not buying water, but deep down he knows that if it doesn't come back into the tapes by Friday night, he is going to have to buy some, as well. Later, on this Friday, about night's fall, in the lower parts of this suburb, it starts trickling through. He knows by about twelve, at night, he would get some. And surely, it comes.

He doesn't simply sleep this night as he fills up every container he has. He contains it in every pot, small dish, big saucers etc... It is feverish collection of this commodity. He is scared at having to face up to having no water. He starts at twelve and by half past five he has collected enough, to last him for nearly two weeks. It seems that's where there are heading towards, realizing reserves for two weeks. It is the new ritual. He wonders if electricity were to start doing that, how he would survive in the ensuing ugliness. The larger fear, what if the tapes dry permanently? Would they go back to the days of learning about the alphabet, fetching it straight from the river?

Chapter 7

2013 Elections Preparedness

Throughout the GNU entity, elections were the talking point, and could happen any moment. Through their discussions and arguments, the players in this GNU entity knew it was the election that was going to decide the way forward for Zimbabwe. The negotiations were for us to have a free and fair election that was credible. For the ZANU-PF, it seemed, all they wanted was a constitution for the election to be done, in a way that recognises them, if they were going to win. They made sure discussions were simply centred on the constitution creation process. They made this process difficult for the opposition, MDC, thus they embroiled the MDC into fights and arguments on this, right to the last day. Thus this process, the ZANU-PF made sure, became the sponge, and it soaked away all the GNU years into it.

In the process, the ZANU-PF, through Mugabe, set several dates for elections, saying, mostly, it depended on the constitution. But sometimes, Mugabe would say they were going to be elections, constitution or no constitution. The next moment the ZANU-PF will then stifle the constitution making process, by embroiling all and sundry over small issues of the constitution, like the gay rights. The ZANU-PF milked this, saying, in the outreach stage; the entire majority of Zimbabweans said they didn't want gay people to have rights. They made the country focus on this issue rather than important issues of governance and elections. In making the country waste their energies on boundary issues, they wasted the GNU time in these than in important issues. Thus issues that had to be thoroughly dealt with, issues like other reforms, ZEC reforms, Security sector reforms, electoral law reforms, media reforms, reconciliation issues and voters roll auditing, were given scant time.

Throughout these constitution making arguments, and through the 5 years of the GNU entity, the ZANU-PF, gave small concessions on these several other issues noted above, just to hoodwink everyone into thinking there were progress on these, but these cosmetic surgery attempts didn't change anything on the political playing field. We eventually had an election with a negotiated constitution, and much of what was obtaining pre-2008 on the other issues.

The MDC thought elections would only happen when they had exhausted all the reforms that needed to be done, thus by the time the election were finally announced and gazetted for 31 July 2013, the MDC was caught unprepared for it. They depended on the good faith of their opponent, in playing fairly, but were duped. It is immaturity on the MDC to think they could depend on the good faith of ZANU-PF. They knew their opponent, over the years; that their opponent never goes out of its way to give their opponent a fair chance, so for the MDC to think things had changed with the ZANU-PF was immature and naivety on their part.

Throughout the GNU life the ZANU-PF were busy campaigning, organising their structures and making the necessary changes to link it back with the electorate, whilst the MDC were busy in the GNU and the negotiations, putting pressure on ZANU-PF to complete the reforms, through canvassing support from SADC, AU, and the international community. So that, 31 July caught them with their pants down. As usual, they run around, to the SADC etc..., trying to stop this election, but what they failed to grasp was that these negotiations were pegged on the willingness of the ZANU-PF to allow for some certain things to happen, for them to have a chance.

The ZANU-PF, whilst on one hand allowed the MDC to push the issue to the SADC discussions platforms, listening to the MDC's grievances, on the other hand, its other important structure to the obstruction of fair play in politics in Zimbabwe, the judiciary, tightened the screws. After all, whether there was a law in Zimbabwe or not, it still had to be interpreted by this partisan branch of the government, the judiciary. They categorically told parties to the agreement that they had the final say in the interpretation of the laws in Zimbabwe. The time of elections were long overdue, especially considering they were over 39 constituencies that didn't have a sitting MP for too long, saying this situation was defrauding these 39 constituents of their rights, for far too long. This issue that should have been solved a long time before, was dragged by this judiciary and the prosecutors, and was eventually used to argue for the case for elections.

Since the GNU was a negotiated government between the three feuding parties, and the judiciary accepted the decisions of this entity for 5 years, I think it was just political gamesmanship for the judiciary to now think they had to decide the destiny of the country. Legally it was their call, but politically it wasn't their call. They should have stayed out and allowed the political process to continue, but they were used by the ZANU-PF as the stick, whilst the ZANU-PF dangled the carrot to the MDC, by allowing discussions to continue at the SADC on the election date decision. Even when the negotiations had agreed for a 2 week extension, to allow for some other reforms, the judiciary were reluctant, thus the election happened on 31 July. Even if the two weeks allowed had been taken into consideration by the players, not much was going to be achieved in those two weeks that these players had failed to do in 5 years of GNU.

So the election happened with just cosmetic changes. At the ZEC, they appointed a new ZEC boss, in Rita Makarau, hoodwinking us into believing they were changes, but the entire workforce of the ZEC were ZANU-PF people. They removed most of the teachers who had carried out election work in the previous elections, and planted ZANU-PF youths, former militias and unofficial security people into this process. I can attest that the ZEC officer I saw, who came for the outreach program before the election, is a ZANU-PF youth coordinator of our district, as well, a CIO agent. I know it because previously we had clashed. In April 2011, he tried to harass and threaten me when he realised I write stuff against the ZANU-PF. It was after he had seen my story, GUKURAHUNDI, on the Matabeleland massacres of the 1980s, posted on a West Indies web magazine, *Wizard4Ebooks*, and I had transported it onto my face book site. He made a lot of threats saying that I shouldn't be writing about that, let alone about anything critical of the government. I asked him who he was to make that directive to me. He brought out his CIO card, and confessed he was a CIO agent. Two years later, he came to my home, as a ZEC official.

So, for the negotiators to think that by just putting a judge as the president of ZEC, and think that she could sort all the problems at this body, in less than three months before elections was self-serving on the part of the ZANU-PF and naive on the part of the MDC. The ZEC chairman had no control, whatsoever, on the day to day working of this organisation. It was the lower officers in this body, who would do the recruitment of the personnel and the day to day running of this organisation, and it was these that the ZANU-PF had full control over, and these officials employed people who leaned to the ZANU-PF party lines.

The next port of call was media reforms. An NGO that focuses on electoral issues in Zimbabwe, ZIMBABWE ELECTION SUPPORT NETWORK (ZESN): in their BALLOT UPDATE, Issue 9: September to October 2012 observes:

Research by Mass Public Opinion Institute (MPOI) has revealed that over 75 per cent of the population relies on state media for information. Organisations such as the Media Monitoring Project of Zimbabwe in their reports have noted the bias in state media in favour of ZANU-PF in terms of voices. ZESN remains concerned that while state media is the most received, it is not well trusted by citizens. ZESN notes that the most problematic aspect with ZBC radio and television is that they do not provide the right of reply to the parties and people they report on particularly the MDC formations. This has led to erosion in trust levels among citizens. It is critical that as Zimbabwe prepares for the referendum and general election it is important that state owned media makes all efforts to be non-partisan and partial towards ZANU-PF and that all parties be provided with the right of reply to issues they will have raised.

Except for the two editions of radios (STAR FM, ad Zi FM), the rest are public broadcasters, who are always pro-ZANU-PF. For the entire GNU period, they had been the ZANU-PF's propaganda mouth pieces, and they changed their coverage and policies only 2 weeks before the election. How can that be fair play, when in 5 years you were just allowed only 2 weeks, where your issues were allowed free airplay, and the rest of the time you were under the hammer, being criticised. Even the 2 private radio stations are just "purportedly" fair. Star FM is owned by the Zimpapers group, which is owned by the state, thus controlled by the ZANU-PF, and Zi FM is owned by a prominent ZANU-PF official, Super Mandiwanzira, who was the candidate for the ZANU-PF, for Nyanga West constituency, who ultimately won it, and is the sitting MP for this place, and now the deputy minister of information and publicity, the ministry that controls the media. To what extend would these two public media were to play toward opening up of the airwaves when they were still controlled by the same system and party?

The only independent Medias are found in the electronic media field, where they are a clutch of independent papers (Newsday, Standard, Zimbabwe Independent, Daily News, and Financial Gazette). These are even fewer than those from the public media group, Zimpapers, so they had little influence on the electorate than the Zimpapers stable. On top of that, the ZANU-PF controlled this ministry through its minister, Webster Shamu, who did the usual thing of threatening and harassing the private media. These few independent media worked in a situation like that of the pre-GNU, with laws like *Access to Information Protection and Privacy Act* (AIPPA) hanging on their heads.

The same individuals in the private newspapers were the same who had witnessed harassments, were beaten and incarcerated over the years. They have been abused, and I feel, they were not doing their jobs without fear and favour. They knew there were things, if they were to report on, they would be in hot soup. The government would just use AIPPA to terrorise them. Such that if you were to check these papers you would feel a shift that has happened over the years, softening their stance on issues against the ZANU-PF. They are no longer confrontational, but report apologetically against the ZANU-PF. For example, the Daily News of Jeff Nyarota of the early 2000 was more investigative, straight shooting, and on the ball than the Daily News of Stanley Gama now. This shouldn't be construed as criticism of these private media, and or Stanley Gama, in fact I have huge respect for him. It is about how this abusive system that was still obtaining, even in the GNU entity, has watered us down, on our want to exercise our democratic citizenship, in various ways. Even the opposition has mellowed down, too, so have the general majority of the Zimbabweans, always afraid of being beaten, killed, harassed, and incarcerated for exercising our rights.

The same lip service given to media reforms was given to the electoral laws and voters roll. The voters roll is in shambles, so are the electoral laws. There is a dire need to start crafting again a new voter's roll, and the electoral laws. The electoral laws that are there still keep the decision making rights in the same people who are part of a flawed justice system, people who have been partisan. I suggest we create a new system whereby the electoral contestation issues are dealt with by a different justice system than that runs the judiciary system in the country. We could make a body that comprise people coming from different sectors of the country, including, of course, from the judiciary. This body should have the final decision on any election and election dispute issue, and are allowed to do their work without fear and favour.

Another issue related to this is of the granting of immunity to people who have made the system corrupt, flawed and in shambles; immunity from prosecution. In doing that we are saying these people are allowed to be above the law, thus even when they don't do their jobs well, they are still unaccountable to the entire country, only to their bosses, who would protect them from non-performance because they have done these bosses service by creating situations that allow these bosses to stay in their jobs. If someone is a public servant, he is answerable to the country, and if he messes at his job, the country should have the right to bring them under scrutiny. We should also have direct control over those who work for us; otherwise if every control mechanism is left in the hands of a few people, or one person, then that person is as good above the laws of the country. There is no sense for issues of dispute of elections to be dealt with by bodies that were created by part-players, part-bosses, or by individuals of whom they rely heavily on, for their survival in the body. These individuals or bodies do not have much choice but to protect those who gave them these jobs. Electoral issues should simply be outside the system. In the last election of 31 July 2013, the judiciary, who were appointed into these benches by the president, were made to decide on a dispute that involved the same person who had appointed them.

In simple terms, it's like at a company situation; if a worker complains of sexual abuse, from his employer, the CEO. The company's rules stipulate that the human resources office should investigate the issue and decide whether there is any grain of truth. How much the human resources would do, knowing that if they were to persecute the CEO, he can fire them from their jobs, begs answers. It's most likely they won't be a fair treatment of this issue, unless the issue is dealt with by an outside body, not answerable to this CEO. It is the problem we have with our legal system that we use for electoral disputes. The one who controls the system will always have an advantage.

In the anthology, *There is No Cholera in Zimbabwe*, Edited by *Jonathan Marcantoni and Zachary M. Oliver* which came out from *Aignos Publishing, Inc, 2013, USA, Emdadul Haque,* in his essay, CONTROVERSY IN BANGLADESH JUDICIARY note and we could borrow from the Bangladesh system whereby a caretaker government is enacted when the election date is promulgated until the election result has been announced and approved. This caretaker government would be running the country, and this would allow the players in the election to remain players only, unlike the system which we have here where a player is also the referee. In Bangladesh the Chief Justice would assume this position until a new government is sworn.

The voters roll was another issue that needed to be dealt with by removing it from the same office (Registrar General) or person who has created a shamble of it, and putting it in the hands of an independent body.

The other issue of reforms that had to be dealt with was on the security sector system. On this one, nothing, whatsoever, was done. There was no security sector leader who lost his job, there was no shuffling of any sort, not even any redirecting, nothing. We went to the election with the same system. To begin with, there were not even any assurances from those security sector leaders who had made political statements on who they would recognise or not, that they would now respect the country's decisions. We went to the election with the possibility of the involvement of the security establishment in the decisions, on deciding who would lead us, hanging on our heads. There were no changes in the laws that had been used by the security sector personnel to abuse, victimise, and kill us..., the laws like AIPPA, *Public Order Security Act* (POSA), etc... Even though we had the new constitution that protected us from abuse, but a constitution is not particular. It's just a general frame. Laws like AIPPA, POSA, were still effective. ZESN, notes,

> Observers in Provinces such as Manicaland, Mashonaland West, Mashonaland Central, Mashonaland East, Harare, Masvingo and Matebeleland North and South have traces of youth militia activities. These are mainly led by the youth officers who are stationed in each ward who are clearly pro- ZANU-PF in their approach yet they are paid through the taxpayers' money. The youth officers are the eyes and ears of ZANU-PF yet they are paid through government funds. It is critical that the role of these youth officers be interrogated more so as the country heads towards elections in which the stakes are high so that Zimbabwe does not degenerate into another violent election (September-October 2012: 7).

A policeman can still arrest you using these laws, i.e. AIPPA, and POSA, even though it could have been an illegal arrest, and once you were arrested, you were at the mercy of these policemen, until your case is brought to the justice system. For some people it has taken several months, some years, for their cases to be heard. Such that, by the time you are acquitted of your charges, you would have gone under inhuman abuse that would never be re-corrected or compensated in any way, at all. There is heavy reliance in our laws on the policemen to interpret laws in matters of arresting a citizen, and reliance on the same policemen in guarding the prisoner's rights until found guilty, which would have been fair had our policemen been fair and impartial professionals. But, our police force is politicised towards the ZANU-PF interests, thus any opposition member found contravening the laws is abused with impunity by this body.

The other important reform that had to be carried out to its entirety is that of national reconciliation and healing. Mapuva (2010: 249) quotes (Saed, 2010):

> It has been realised that rebuilding a country after civil strife is not only about re-building visible infrastructure, but rebuilding emotional healing and stress management. The exercise also involves a situation where one could envisage the myriad activities and challenges that need to be addressed to restrain the possibility of war-relapse. Peace-building cannot be viewed simply as a "quick-fix-strategy" applied to people who will have witnessed unrest or in failed states that are experiencing dysfunction in their structures and strategies. Peace-building initiatives, practices and procedures require a multi-faceted approach working to achieve "positive peace" in every aspect of social life.

Zimbabwe, in simple terms, is full of people who should have been hospitalized but were made to deal with their own wounds on their own. It goes back to those who were born before independence. These were made to go through life changing situations by the war. I was 7 when we got independent, and what I know of that time, and that has stayed with me up to now, is nights on end when we were made to sleep outside, in the bushes, and of the sounds of guns, the red arrows of bullets by night, the crazy death sounds all around us, the endless runs. There were days on end we were made to run from our homes, sometimes during daylight, the beatings, killings, the total chaotic situation. It's not fair for someone to think, a seven old who is subjected to that would ever be normal. We can only try to be normal, but we can never be really normal. The same applies to those who were older, those who had been crippled, those who had relatives killed, and those who were abused by the system obtaining. This applies for those who underwent the same inhumanity during the Gukurahundi massacres, which was even a lot devastating, for those who had relatives killed for no apparent reason at all, in a purportedly free country. There are also those who were abused and killed in the militarisation of the country post-2000, and those many unknown who died for other political misdemeanours pre-2000. It's a lot of people, and one can easily say; it's the whole country. Everyone has been at the receiving end of injustice, abuse, killings, victimisation etc...

So that, what we have is a country that has been made into cripples, I don't only mean physical cripples, I mean emotional cripples, as well. Emotionally crippled is the harder of the two because you don't know how to deal with it or its influences, some of which are beyond your grasp. We need an open hospital, which is open to everyone. We can't all afford the services of psychiatric treatment in the hospitals, so we need an open hospital, in the form of reconciliation and national healing, even bigger than the South African one. Our wounds go back to pre-liberation wars, and up to this moment of writing, so we need this issue to be dealt with on a bigger scale than the South African one. The other reason is that, unlike the South African issue in which the reconciliation programme was centred on one system or people hurting the other, I mean, generally speaking, the white apartheid system against the blacks and other fringe races. Ours goes beyond that because

71

there has been black against black abuses, for over 30 years, on top of the white against black of pre-liberation, and also we witnessed two wars, one of which dragged for over 20 years. South Africa was never really in a war situation, like us. It means our abuse and victimisation was all pervasive and corrosive.

What this means is that we went to an election with a hospital load of the electorate. People who were afraid and didn't trust the system that was running the election, because these same people had victimised, abused, killed, and maimed us. Our minds were not free of the fear, anger, and mistrust of this system. A lot of people didn't just do anything, I mean they didn't vote. Some people had just given up on the whole system. Why vote, when in their psyche, they know it would be a stolen election, when they know they won't be real change, when they know they will always be victims. To them they are always victims, and this victim syndrome is so embedded into them, that it would require a system of rehabilitation, a rehabilitation in which they have control over. That would allow them to start participating, let alone unshackle themselves off this victim's posture. The reconciliation and national healing done was just as piecemeal an event, like the media and ZEC reforms. It was done on the surface. We were left alone, still hurting, not knowing what to do to fix ourselves. We are still forced to stay in the same area with our abusers, who continuously flaunt their strength and power over us. How are we supposed to heal when we haven't been helped in letting go off our pains and hurts?

Other reforms that never gained much ground were the reformation of the entire base system of our governance. The whole system is full of the ZANU-PF people, and it would have taken more than just the 5 years of the GNU years to level it out. It is this base system that run things in Zimbabwe. A minister in a ministry simply deals with strategic issues, not tactical, day to day running of a ministry. This is left in the hands of the permanent secretaries, directors of departments, managers, etc. These, who have been in the employ of the same government, have aligned themselves to the ZANU-PF, such that the ZANU-PF still controlled the running of all ministries during the GNU time and elections. The same applies to governors of the provinces who also control the provincial government structures, like provincial, district, ward administrators. The same applied to ambassadors, and governors or directors of different state organs who were answerable to the ZANU-PF, and ultimately to the president. Nothing much happened in the 5 years of the GNU to shake that system to create professionalism and fairness. We went to an election with a system which was hugely flawed, and sided with the ZANU-PF.

So that, in the people's minds, there was cheating. It starts straight away from this mistrust that we have of a system that is corrupt and partisan, which is made to preside over our decisions every time. That's why groups or people like Baba Jukwa, Mai Jukwa, and theories of an Israeli election rigging organisation, Nikuv, were the main news of our mistrust of this system. I still don't believe Baba Jukwa knew what was really happening in the system as he purportedly claimed. He gave us one or two pointers such that we became so focused on his statements, and forgot the larger issue was to go and vote, all of us. We thought he would tell us everything that was happening. He even told us the government, and ZANU-PF was fractured to the extent that it won't be possible for it to field candidates, to do any election at all, let alone for the ZANU-PF to win it. We believed him, and in our hundreds of thousands we followed him. So did we follow other forms of him, like Mai Jukwa etc...

If really this Israeli firm rigged our election, then why didn't Baba Jukwa tell us about this and exposed it before it had happened? He claimed to know everything. People started giving credence to the rigging of the election, by this Israeli body, about the Election Day, and post-election. Why something wasn't known to stop it before the election? Not that I really believe there was such huge rigging by this body. I am not saying there totally were no rigging. Yes, it might have happened, maybe not just by this body alone. It's the entire system that is flawed that allows anyone who controls a structure to use it to rig with it. But the said rigging was not going to change the general election result. The ZANU-PF was winning this election, with or without rigging. The majority of people in Zimbabwe were now behind the ZANU-PF, I mean those who wanted to vote and have always voted. There were three poll forecasting and think-houses who had since predicted a ZANU-PF win, including Freedom House.

The MDC had lost contact with its people, so whatever rigging that happened might only have made the ZANU-PF get the two thirds majorities in the parliament. But winning they were winning this election. They had done their job well. All this furore about Baba Jukwa, Mai Jukwa, and the Israeli firm, etc. were things that were created to feed into the psyche of the people who didn't believe in the system, maybe by the same system that wanted to stay intact. I can't believe, even up to now, the government doesn't know who Baba Jukwa is or was. These are the other side games we were made to play, so as to not focus on the important thing, that is, we had to go and vote. Some people didn't go and vote because Baba Jukwa had told them there was going to be rigging. Some people didn't go and vote because they were afraid of rumours awash of a coup two weeks before the elections, some of the impending coup if the country were going to boot the ZANU-PF out of office. *As I have noted before that I wrote this book just after the election. I would like to note now that it has been brought to light that the said Baba Jukwa was a ZANUPF-PF plot created by ministers Jonathan Moyo and Savious Kasukuwere and a Sunday Mail (part of the Zimpapers group) newsman.*

I got to two weeks before the election date unbelieving of it. In me there was still this sense that it wasn't going to happen. It was like the hyperrealism of Baudrilard's simulacra theories. The MDC started campaigning seriously in those few days, and tried all their best, but it wasn't good enough, to cover the whole country. For a party to be expected to do its job, that it should have done in 5 years, in 2 weeks, is just a big joke. That's why I have argued, all throughout the book, the MDC were caught napping with this election. And, they are primarily to blame for this. They put their fate in the good nature of someone else, rather than doing their job and wait for this good nature, they made it the basis of their outlook. By now, they should have learned that the ZANU-PF would never do reforms that would make them weak. These security sector reforms, ZEC reforms, Media reforms were going to make them weak. In the 2007 mediation for the 2008 election, by Thabo Mbeki, ZANU-PF hoodwinked the country by making piecemeal reforms, as well. Bratton and Masunungure (2011: 30) note,

In December 2007, the ZANU-PF government announced piecemeal legislative reforms to POSA (to allow political rallies as long as police deemed no threat of violence) and the Broadcasting Services Act (to guarantee balanced coverage of election campaigns and selectively allow licencing of journalists and broadcasters). No sooner had agreement been reached, however, than Mugabe unilaterally declared a timetable for elections on March 29, 2008 without addressing MDC's precondition of comprehensive constitutional reform. Moreover, as soon became apparent, ZANU-PF did not intend to abide by the new laws: the police continued to block or harass opposition gatherings and the government-controlled media continued to praise the ruling party and castigate the opposition, if it covered their activities at all. And the ruling party– intent on bolstering its main social base among the peasantry – turned traditional leaders into appendages of the ruling party. Pampered with development services and consumer goods, the chiefs were expected to act as the eyes and ears of ZANU-PF in the locality and to deliver the rural vote (or, if necessary, coercively extracting it) in a typical clientelistic relationship.

This is what Mugabe did again, in July 2013. Once he got the constitution, and made piecemeal reforms to ZEC, media, voters roll, he called for an election, even though nothing much had changed, knowing he still had control of every apparatus of governance. Someone might argue that if Mugabe won the election because he was in control of apparatus such as media, voters roll etc., so the MDC didn't lose the election because they didn't give themselves time enough to connect with the electorate. Thus one would say MDC-T lost because ZANU-PF was in control of the system. I still insist the MDC-T should have done their job first, whether reforms or no reforms, as they have always done in the previous elections where these systems were even a lot more lopsided to the side of the ZANU-PF. Thus I would still maintain that the biggest reason the MDC-T lost the election was they had lost touch with their electorate, unlike pre-2008 where even though the playing field was a lot lopsided to the side of the ZANU-PF, the MDC-T still kept in touch with its electorate. ZANU-PF, just like in the previous elections used the media to get in touch with the electorate. Thus I am saying ZANU-PF still did their job unlike the MDC-T who didn't.

I want to explore this allegation of an Israeli firm being involved in our vote, rigging it for the ZANU-PF. Unless, this firm was working outside the government to government agreements between Israel and Zimbabwe, it couldn't have been possible. But if this information or arrangement was known by the Israeli government, I find it difficult to believe it.

The USA which everyone knows supports the opposition movement in Zimbabwe is a very close ally of Israel. The USA can afford to disagree with Britain (several instances in the UN structures) over Israel blatant abuse system and behaviour in the Middle East. So, how come the Israeli government would have allowed a situation whereby the USA foreign policy and interests were disturbed by a firm that has Israelis in its leadership? Not only that; a firm that is registered in Israel, has offices in Israel, a firm known for specialising in elections (ultimately governance) issues in other countries. Why both the governments, up to now, I mean the USA and Israeli, haven't had talks or corrective measures against that, or even imposition of sanctions against this firm by the USA. I believe the Israeli government's relationship or foreign policy friendship with the USA is more important than that with Zimbabwe so Israel should be respectful of the United States' interest in Zimbabwe better than its interests in Zimbabwe.

Suppose someone might still maintain that this said firm did indeed stole the vote, and that it was working outside government to government bilateral agreements between Zimbabwe and Israel. Yes, it is possible, but the questions still begs. If they were real time evidence from the MDC that this firm had stolen the election, why didn't they partition courts in Israel for this firm to be brought to book, or even United Nations courts, or even ours. It was even confusing why, after the MDC had been refused the right to bring ZEC and Registrar General to court they withdrew their court case? Why didn't they continue with litigation, just to expose these regularities? We all know that justice was far-fetched but politics doesn't only deal with justice, for public opinion is more potent than getting justice in the situation we are in. So pursuing the court case was important and should have been done to completion.

It has become this funny fictional game with the opposition to cry foul every time they are beaten at an election.

In the discussions I have had with the national youth chairperson of the MDC-N, Gideon Mandaza, a church mate and old friend, on this vote-rigging by the Nikuv. I asked him to explain to me how this firm purportedly rigged the election in his constituency, in Zengeza West constituency, where the MDC-T candidate won by less than 100 votes. I could understand rigging being rife in rural areas where most of the opposition parties have not enough monitors or control of. But in the third biggest city, right there under their sights, it is difficult to justify why the MDC won with less than 100 votes, yet in the same constituency, going back to 10-15 years ago it used to win with plus 10000 more votes than ZANU-PF. The same happened in a lot of the urban seats the MDC won, and those that the ZANU-PF wrestled away from the MDC. The gap is now very small. I will deal with this phenomenon in the next two chapters. I also asked him whether they were times they left the polling stations unattended, he said, "no". He said when they went to eat, they locked all the doors, boxes etc..., and also their security people were outside the polling station building securing the place. When they returned back they checked everything. Nothing had been broken into. He was still baffled how the rigging could have happened under those conditions, as well, but still maintained it happened. This is what I can't seem to understand and accept.

It would be unfair not to note some of the rigging tactics that were said to be employed. There was a systematic transferring of people from their usual voting wards to a ward far away, such that those people didn't vote. There was the issue of the voter's slip that was abused, with some saying there were over 4000 people planted throughout Zimbabwe who were running this scheme, of using these voters slip, giving to several people one same slip to vote in different places throughout the country, it could be on ward, constituent or province basis. This was unearthed by Tendai Biti, and the newspapers (Daily News), when people had been bussed to vote in Biti's constituency of Mt Pleasant, with fake voter's slip. These were people who were coming from outside that constituency. It is one of the reasons I argued the voter's roll needed to be disbanded and we start new registration. These people, who had registered on the 2013 outreach, some couple or so months before the election, didn't have their names in the voters roll by the time we got to an election, so they were unaccountable, and voted using slips. If you had access to the voter slip, and you could even create your own voter's slips, and still use them for voting, and it was all up to you how many times you would do that. We don't know, up to now how many times each of these voter's slips were used. From what was gleaned, people were being paid 10 dollars to do this. The ink is not a problem; it can be cleaned beyond the scrutiny of human eye. There were no machines to determine whether one had voted before, through analysing the ink electronically by machines.

Another aspect of voter rigging that was alleged to also have been employed was there were several boxes with voted slips that were said to have been smuggled into the polling stations, especially in rural areas. For those who could calculate, they felt with the pace of voting, it was not possible for a constituency to have over 23 000 votes inside a day. I won't substantiate this allegation, just like I can't validate the suggestion that the papers we used to vote that were allegedly supplied by the noted above Israeli firm, had been infused with some watermark ink, such that when you vote, your ink will be transported (I don't even know by whatever process) onto the ZANU-PF candidate position, such that most of the opposition votes ended up being ZANU-PF votes. These are just speculations that I can't substantiate. I am sure, just like in previous election periods, there were many other irregularities and rigging tactics used. It is simply difficult for anyone to start believing that the ZANU-PF exercised fair play. It's deeply embedded in us that the ZANU-PF cheats, so in our minds, it cheated, even though factually nothing much of that sort could have happened to change the direction of the vote.

This mistrust is evidenced by the fact that when the election results news begun sneaking throughout the country, of the ZANU-PF sweeping over the seat, especially in hugely MDC's strongholds, people started talking of all the above rigging tactics. When it had hit them squarely that the ZANU-PF was winning, people became so quiet, devastated, angry, and hurt. I have never seen such pain on the people's faces; especially on people from the urban areas. It was more than the despondence, devastated, painful postures I have come to see on people's faces, when the national soccer team has failed, at the last hurdle, to qualify for an important tournament. It was just all pervasive darkness that descended on the people.

It took about 4 days for people to start voicing their displeasures with the election result, to start dealing with the pain. At that instant I realised we were lost. We also realised we were bereft of any ideas to make us move on with our lives. Straight away, I told myself and friends that I was leaving the country, for good. But, I haven't been able to do so, up to now. Despite not succeeding leaving this country, I am still trying to figure out whether there is anything worth fighting for in this country. Writing this book, is a way to finding the way forward for me, and the country. Considering that we have hit the bottom, in a really hard way, it would take an incredible, undying spirit from all of us to start the journey again, or to find a way again.

Chapter 8

The Lost Dream

Participating in a democracy requires putting one's life and trust on the good faith of others. For Mandela and the ANC to participate in the negotiations for multi-party democracy, with the apartheid authority in South Africa, in the 1990s, they had to have faith in that apartheid entity to negotiate in good faith. This is what we, in Zimbabwe, have been staking our lives and trust on, the good faith of the ZANU-PF, for all our post-independence life. Every time, we have our faith trampled on. Every time we go to these elections with faith and high hopes that we are going to have free and fair elections, and every time we have been crying. In this chapter, and the whole book, I am trying to deconstruct what has been undemocratic, what has been bad faith of others, of us, of you, of me, and try to put out the real, the ideal through this deconstruction. It is like a fire gospel (James Baldwin called it, "The fire next time"), urging you, me or everyone who want to see democracy, I mean multi-party democracy, based on social justice and equality before the law, back in Zimbabwe, to now stand up and fight.

The price of freedom is not cheap, and there is no price for culpable ignorance. When you say you won't go and vote because already the election is lost, I find determinism in this, a defeatist attitude. Determinism is the notion that all events follow a natural law, therefore humans have no say in their fate or destiny. Why not just die! This determinism, this defeatist attitude that we have already lost an election before the first pen scribbles the ballot influences on the group's, and ultimately, on the whole country's psychology. It encourages a defeatist attitude which leads to self-fulfilling prophecies- ideas that become reality because simply one believes them. It creates the myth of paradise as always lost- a movement not towards it, but away from it. As a country, as a people, we are blanketed in this attitude now. We are defeated. We have defeated ourselves. We cry, we are always crying babies, and we can't just stand up and confront our bear and perish, or succeed.

They were slightly over 6 million people on Zimbabwe's voter's roll, but over 2 million voted for Mugabe, and over 1 million voted for Tsvangirai, and the question is, where the other 3 million were. Why didn't they face the bear and perish with others. No, they were already defeated before the date for elections was announced. Time for excuses is long gone. I am calling you up, to stand up and fight for your destiny. You should have taken a couple of days leave at your workplace in South Africa, the UK, Botswana, and come and cast your ballot, but you chose the defeatist attitude and, assumed others were going to curve out a destiny for you. You should have asked your professor, your director of studies, at the university you are in, for a couple of days, to come and cast your ballot for this country you so love. You should have taken time out from your religious work, prayers, duties and come and vote. My parish priest, Joseph Matare, told us a couple of days before voting, that when you are eligible to vote, and you don't vote for no apparent reason, you commit a social sin. By not voting, he said you allow or chose a destiny for those who are incapable (under 18), a destiny that might be of suffering (exactly what is obtaining here), and it's a social sin you have caused on those who were not yet able to vote. That there are school going children who are out of school, who can't afford school fees, children who can't afford basic healthcare, shelter and food, is because you didn't exercise your democratic citizenship.

You should have gone to register to vote, if you were 18 years old and above. You should have done that way before the

82

elections, for voter registration is an ongoing activity. On the Election Day you had no excuse. A lot of young people between the ages of 18-30 years old were unregistered, despite campaigns done to entice them to register, so they didn't vote. It's the thinking of the defeatist in them that they have chosen this destiny for themselves. And, to substantiate it more, a lot of these young people who had registered voted for the ZANU-PF, despite the fact that they were jobless, and are still jobless, because of this party's policies. They were promised jobs, and given some money, 10 dollars to disturb the whole process, to steal the destiny from themselves and for the whole country. For only 10 dollars, thousands of these young people voted in several voting wards and constituencies, using the easily produced voter's slips. And now they are littering the streets, jobless, defeated.

This defeated attitude is now the attitude of the whole country. It's the donor money people now care about. It's like a hospital of addicts, donor money addicts. The country is now proliferating with groups, NGOs, parties... etc. of donor money addicts, not people who really want to change their destiny. The opposition party, the MDC, is the biggest group of addicts of this donor money, that's why every Tom, Dick and Harry, and not to forget Charlie, comes into this party, even from outside the country, knowing they could get a bite of money and leadership if they buy this party's ticket. They have lost the direction, and the country has subsequently lost direction. Our dream is lost. All that we now do is waste time in crying, pell-mell, in foreign media, looking for empathy and drug money, but we had an opportunity to change the destiny of our country, for some many years now, and we always failed because we are disorganised.

The ZANU-PF people know what they want, and they always win. Old people, in their 80s in this party, can travel from their plots to their wards to vote, but you are 25 and don't even bother registering, or voting. Yet, it's the young, who constitute the majority in this country, and it's their destiny that's being decided with these elections, but it's these young people who don't want to be shapers of their own destiny. They don't simply care. It's time to tell ourselves there are no more excuses, we are just cowards.

This is even problematic when Zimbabwe is still being considered the most literate country on the continent. The Zimbabweans, all over the world, get good jobs where ever they are because of our education system. We brag endless about this to anyone who can listen to us, but we just can't seem to decide on this important aspect of our destiny. We just can't exercise our democratic citizenship and rights. We are cowards, we are educated fools. This education we brag about is not good enough. It has only made us cowards and "yes" men.

If you voted on 31 July 2013, and your party failed, don't join in this defeatist attitude. Go and vote again and again until you cross the river Jordan. Go out there, and in the next 5 years, talk to those defeated; tell them they have to stand up for their destiny. Tell them to get into this small place between the rock and a hard place where you are. It is a small wedge where they can find real meaning, of their existences and identity, where they can find other real people, real situations, and real destinies. It is time to stand up. We only have seconds to pray now. We only have minutes to meditate. We only have hours to hallucinate. We only have days to end this, to sleepwalk into this destined danger. Our dreams have been burned alive, our fortunes stolen, our promises poisoned.

Get down into the trenches with others, fighting for just a smile. It's us versus them on the hills of hell's eternal massacre. It's us, it is you, and it is me. It's you who voted for the MDC, or ZANU-PF. It's always our butchered dreams. Think of the people who lost their lives for us to have these dreams, people who were maimed. You have an obligation to these people. It's our destiny, our dreams to have multi-party democracy in our country, which seemed to have died. We had arrived at the cusps in 2008, now we are down in the bowls where we came from.

It's wrong for us to give someone over two thirds majority vote to decide our destiny, someone who has been the biggest culprit. It's a handicap. It is wrong to think the country's destiny should be in the hands of one party. It's the MDC and ZANU-PF who have killed this dream, for you and me, who have failed us. It is the truth, the knowledge kicking the beat in our hearts, which now matters. We can go to war, to our own war now, a knowledge war with their divide and conquer attitude and rule. They don't want us to be united in deciding our own destiny. They want to stay in their enriching positions, always making us the poorer. Let us now recover our dream.

Chapter 9

The Urgency Of Now: Alternative Opposition Political Party and Dispensation

We have hit the crossroads as a country, as a people. All that we need is to figure out a way forward. Where we are at is at the edge. It has been a long journey, all through the years, and we were so determined to create a destiny we wanted, a destiny we wanted for our children. It's easier to just say we are lost. We are on the crossroads, not knowing which way to go. But, deep down us we still know what our destination was, but it's the way to or the path to it that we don't know anymore. For years we have supported anything that we have thought could take us to that destination, and time after time we have found ourselves not any closer to the destination, but time after time we have stood up, and embraced the challenge to keep walking towards our destination. We have put so much trust in the MDC entity to deliver us across the line, yet it seems they are disintegrating. They have lost the way, and we are left distraught and bereft of ideas. It is now our obligation to chart the new path, with or without the MDC.

They are a number of scenarios we might or might not have to take to get us through. The first is for us, the electorate who have supported the MDC, over the years, all of us who are tired of the ZANU-PF hegemony over our country, destiny and lives, to ask the MDC to respect our support of them, for them to understand it is us who have fought this battle for them. We have to demand that they start focusing on us again. We want them to come back into our small communities, and work with us on the grassroots. We want the MDC to start articulating our values, of corruption free societies, of fair and free elections and governance, of respect and dignity, for a social contract with us. We have to ask them not to side with capitalist and big money as they have done now. We want the MDC to start listening to us, to let us lead them to where we want to go as a nation, to earn our trust again. This is the first thing the MDC has to do, to get to that respectful relationship it had with us from its start.

There is a camp in the MDC who now believe the way to go is for them to purge some leaders out of their leadership positions, and they have connived with the Western nations to defraud us of the last election, through strangling the MDC financially. In the *Daily News* of 27 January 2014, *Fungai Kwaramba* unearths plots to topple the MDC leader, Tsvangirai, from his position, which they started doing prior the 31 July elections, and have strangled the MDC financially. Tsvangirai was given a paltry $120 000 for campaigning, against Mugabe's over $100 million war chest. It's a misguided attempt, and it would result in another schism as that of the 2005, which saw the MDC breaking up into two camps, thereby weakening it further, and generally the opposition will become more fragmented. This is one thing we have to resist from happening in the next 5 years. There is need for people in the MDC to sit down, and map a way forward together as one party.

I am not saying they are leaders that do not have to go. They should go if they really have to go. Let's be careful we are not going to throw the baby with the bathwater. This camp that has been calling for the MDC president to go is important, even that it is happening now. This camp, purportedly led by Tendai Biti is important in finding a solution to this party's problems. But, the fight has to happen inside the party without a break up. If Tendai Biti feels he has the right to lead this party, he should fight for leadership of this party from the inside. He has to come face to face with Tsvangirai and beat him in a congress. He should now come out in the open and let us know what his intentions are.

There are positives from both leaders if the fight happens inside, and if both sets allow for fair play in this fight. It would prove to all and sundry that indeed the MDC is democratic, where everyone has the right to fight for a position they feel they deserve, and are allowed fair play to fight for the position. If Tsvangirai wins, it would rejuvenate him and put to rest arguments that he has lost direction and the vote. It would garner respect with the donors and foreign governments, let alone, with his subordinates. If he loses he has to accept, peacefully, that he is no longer the chosen one. We will go to a presidential election knowing what and whom the people really want to lead them. If Biti wins, it would give him a lot of confidence. It would be a huge psychological boast for those who have doubted he has what it takes to fill the shoes of the president of the MDC, not just of Tsvangirai. All and sundry will respect him, even Mugabe, whom I feel don't fear Biti, with the support to this project of the break-up of the MDC that ZANU-PF seem to be giving. Mugabe would now realise that even Biti would be a formidable opponent for him, and that he is very much capable. If Biti fails, it would put to rest his ambitions for the time being. It's his ambition to be the president of the MDC that has affected, both positively and negatively, the MDC for some time, from pre-2008 election. His failure to upstage Tsvangirai would put to rest all Tsvangirai's subordinates' ambitions, in the meanwhile, and would allow all these to band together for Tsvangirai, without doubts over his capabilities. This can only happen if it happens in a congress, in a free and fair way.

Going forward, it is important we get to this without the MDC breaking up again. The ball is in both these two leaders' courts to understand that the MDC is bigger than them, and should be preserved at all costs. That applies to everyone who still wants to see multi-party democracy in Zimbabwe, including the Western nations. The break-up of the MDC is a negative thing towards this. Lessons should have been learned by the break-up of 2005, which fragmented the opposition. This time these feuding politicians should put their egos in sheathe, and their coveting of donor monies. It's the altruistic, universal, holistic needs of the people and the country that are important here. It was unnecessary for the MDC to break-up in 2005, it is unnecessary for it to break even now. The break-up of 2005 shouldn't have happened, or been allowed to happen. Bratton and Masunungure (2011: 45) were of the same opinion,

> Even so, the MDC break-up, which was motivated more by personal political ambition than real policy differences, has split the opposition vote and hampered reformers from presenting a clear alternative to ZANU-PF. Both formations (but mainly the MDC-T) suffered heavily during the April-June 2008 run-off election period, when their leaders were scattered outside the country or were intimidated, abducted or killed by the agents of the state. As a consequence, party structures are presently weak, and, like those of ZANU-PF, must be rebuilt.

What they disagreed over wasn't worth breaking-up for. Hell, senators or no senators, the ZANU-PF was winning and still won and both the MDC camps lost out through this break-up. Efforts should now be on re-uniting the whole opposition entity in Zimbabwe into one entity, not another break-up. It's the MDC's structures, which are weak that made them lose the July 31, 2013 election, and it is on this the focus should be on, going forward. So, I am firmly behind those who are calling for reorganisation and reformation of the structures before any election of its leadership.

The MDC should learn from their opponent, ZANU-PF, it simply doesn't break-up, despite disagreements, or weaknesses. If the ZANU-PF gets to a point where they might break-up, they try to not break. The examples are there. In the 2007 congress, in Goromonzi, there were sharp differences in its body politic over whether it was right, as suggested by Mugabe, that the presidential election had to be pushed to 2010 to coincide with the parliamentary and local government elections. Mugabe wanted to use this gimmick to stay in power by amending the constitution, to even push the term for the presidency to 6 years, but the congress voted against that. Mugabe had to respect this decision, or else he would have caused the party to break-up over that. He allowed the fight to continue inside the party by respecting this position. The other instances in which the party could have broken up, which he or the party managed well, were the Tsholotsho declaration, and the wiki leaks debacle. These embroiled the biggest membership of the party's leadership, in meetings to remove Mugabe or to upstage him. The politburo's decision on the wiki leaks debacle was a lesson for all. They said it was not pursuing the issue because they felt it would break the party, and that it was unnecessary. These three examples were huge break-up points than the MDC's break-up issue of 2005, but ZANU-PF stayed united up to now, and won the last election. It's what the opposition should learn from ZANU-PF, and do now.

Much as Tsvangirai has failed, time and again, much as I want to throw him out with the bathwater, in this essay or the entire book, there are huge negatives of Tsvangirai's demise. At the least, it should happen by the books to minimise on these.

It doesn't just take one election period to create a leader who would be able to challenge entrenched despots. They need to have time to mature, as they fight the system. The truth is, it's not a fight against Mugabe, but the system. It has to happen over many years. Tsvangirai has been in the trench for a long time, such that he knows his opponent better than any other leader we might think has better value on paper. He knows his own weaknesses; he knows his own strengths, so do his opponents. He has also worked closely with his opponent for the last five years. It's not little. It's fair to say whatever gains we made in the GNU entity, Tsvangirai was responsible for bringing these about, through his close working, influencing, and control of the president, Mugabe. For him to work with Mugabe for five years without quitting and after failing to win; to still stay outside the government is commendable. Preceding and after the elections, it was common talk that the president had asked Tsvangirai to work with him, and had promised him one of the vice-presidents positions, but he didn't bite. It shows a person who is still ready and willing to fight some more. No amount of cajoling and enriching of the snoot by the Western funders would make him bite this time.

There is also a very important aspect we have to be aware of. It's the psychological space that Tsvangirai has created in every person who has been his supporter over the years. It's like trying to replace the late Yasser Arafat, in his heydays, with Mohammed Abbas, in the Palestine. Even decades after the death of Yasser Arafat, I feel there is no other Palestinian leader who can, and has been able to occupy that psychological space Yasser Arafat left. The MDC has been pretty much about Tsvangirai. It's this space I think any other of his lieutenants (Tendai Biti, Nelson Chamisa, Elton Mangoma, etc.) would struggle to create with the electorate, not in one election period, unless they are going out there and be so radical. Even more radical than Tsvangirai ever was, or even thought he could ever be. I don't even know to what extent they could go to make a dent in the ZANU-PF's fortunes. It simply won't be a stroll in the park.

Suppose we are to take this path, now should be the time to decide on this leader. This leader should be given enough time to really get into the face of the ZANU-PF. He needs more time to prepare the ground, to start pushing the ZANU-PF; back into response-mode it was all those years ago. I suggest that, with that intention in mind, and if it should be agreed upon by the MDC, they should push the congress forward to this year, 2014 or to next year, to sort these leadership problems before they become a cancer to the MDC. A solution should be found as soon as possible, for prolonging these squabbles is unhealthy to the party, and would provide theatre and fodder for the public media and ZANU-PF to keep tinkering into the MDC's internal issues.

Another way to go is for the two protagonists to sit down and iron out their differences. I believe it's just their personal differences, over the years, that has added to the two's disconnection. They might need to sit down and figure out whether they really do have real differences. Their differences could have sprouted from the following, according to Knox Chitiyo, in his book, A CASE FOR SECURITY SECTOR REFORMS IN ZIMBABWE (2009: 23),

> The decision on whether to join the GNU or not was bitterly divisive within the MDC National Executive, and among supporters. The MDC's inability to end political repression, stop land invasions, or oust Gideon Gono from the Reserve Bank, continues to alienate the radical wing of the party.

There is also need to work hard to strengthen the MDC's top 3-7 positions; president, vice-president, chairperson, secretary general, organising secretary, treasurer general, chief spokesman. The treasurer general, going by the accusations that it sabotaged Tsvangirai's last election campaigns, by making available a paltry $120 000 against Mugabe's war chest of $100 million, and many other accusations of financial strangling of Tsvangirai so that they could push for his ouster, thus this position needs working on.

The two secretary positions (general secretary and organising secretary) are the point entry and engagement with the electorate positions. They manage the structures, and action of the party. And these, it seems, no longer have a close touch with the electorate. There is a breakdown in communication or relationship between the MDC, and the people who have always voted for them, let alone between those at Harvest house (MDC headquarters) and those who were in the government, thus this breakdown is due to the malfunctioning of the two secretary positions.

The national chairperson is invisible. You can forget the party has that position, and the other two invisible positions are those of the vice-president and that of chief spokesperson. That the MDC has been embroiled in scandals, like Tsvangirai's love and marriage escapades and those of the councillors' corruption and mismanagement of urban and local authorities is because of the malfunctioning of these positions. These three positions are important in managing these situations but failed, even in spin-doctoring these situations so that the public media and the ZANU-PF couldn't make a meal over.

I want to delve on the vice-president position which should be the most powerful position in the MDC, because it is the link between Tsvangirai, and the rest of executive and ultimately the whole party and the electorate. In the Western nations' thinking that the MDC should have a vibrant, in-your-face leader in Biti, and other than taking Biti to the presidency in a move that would break the party, why not push Tsvangirai to be like Biti. Yes, an old dog can be retrained. We keep Biti at his position, working hard to rectify his limitations at his position, of re-engaging with the people.

I can't use this thinking on the vice-president, spokesperson, and national chairperson positions. To strengthen Tsvangirai we need these positions to be stronger, but we can't train all these people. Maybe we need new people on those positions. We need a radical, fearless, straight-shooter vice-president. We need someone very visible, politically speaking. We might need people like Priscilla Misihayirambwi Mushonga, Theresa Makoni, Sekai Holland. If the person has to come from Matabeleland, let's find someone from that region who would make that position interesting; a person who could fare well against their opposite in the ZANU-PF, Joyce Mujuru. I am sorry to say Thokozani Khupe is just not interesting. Check the George Bush presidency. It was simply managed by his very powerful vice-president, Dick Chaney.

The vice-president position is the position people would check on, too, in the choice of the president. People talk a lot about this position; they want an interesting and attractive personality in this position. Consider on how much there is so much talk about Mujuru, and nothing much about Khupe. There is now no doubt, in people's minds, that Mujuru could take over from Mugabe, and make all the best of this job, than say, would people think about Khupe. These are some of the issues and positions that need working on in this leadership renewal take.

The Western nations, and partly the ruling party are moving for the ouster of the MDC leader, and the fact that the ZANU-PF is interested in this project, should be a pointer to the faction pushing for the ouster of Tsvangirai, that if this move is being taken as a good move by the ruling party, then it is not good for the MDC. The ZANU-PF doesn't support something they feel will hurt them. They know of the permanent threat of Tsvangirai, even when he is down. He has the huge respect of the people, and it's something the ZANU-PF is still scared of. The truth is the MDC didn't win the election, not mainly because of Tsvangirai. The numbers are a pointer.

In the 2008 election Mugabe got slightly over 2 million votes, and he still got over 2 million votes this time. It's the MDC's vote that has waned, mostly because a lot of the opposition's support left for other countries after the March election, in 2008. When we really hit the bottom in 2008, a lot of people left. I left too, but I am back, yet a lot of people never returned back, that's primarily why his support went down from over 2 million to over a million. The MDC has been blind to this and never bothered to try to replace this chunk of votes that left (just checking my street or close relatives, the bulk of people who are over 18 years old and have the legal right to register for voting are not even registered in Zimbabwe to vote, and mostly these are between 18-30 years old). The MDC never tried to make those who left Zimbabwe to return for the vote, or even to fight for the outside electorate to have the right to vote. If the outside electorate had been allowed to vote, especially in big Zimbabwean population countries like Botswana, South Africa, and the UK, ZANU-PF had no chance against the MDC, rigging or no rigging. Even the rigging was going to be difficult for ZANU-PF to accomplish because it would have to be done in huge proportions, and needed more days to achieve on. But, the MDC, unknowingly agreed with the ZANU-PF to defraud this entity of its right to democratic citizenship. It's another huge mistake the MDC made by accepting that.

I am saying, baring the foolish love and marriage escapades of the MDC leader, the votes and voting patterns changed through this phenomenon. The most viable way to go with Tsvangirai as the president is for the opposition party to focus on curbing his gaffs, his stupid mistakes, and make him stronger. They have to exercise point management of his private and public lives. Cutting him out can only weaken the opposition. I think the opposition party leaders have to start being selfless, and concentrate on working for the altruistic needs of the people. They should simply all unite in only one front. It's time for us to tell all these opposition parties that they should unite, and have a bite at the ZANU-PF as one force, not as several, confused, barking and whinnying dogs, that do not have any bite at all. It's time for the likes of Job Sikala, professor Welshman Ncube, David Coltart, Ndumiso Ndabengwa, Simba Makoni, professor Arthur Mutambara, professor Lovemore Madhuku, Morgan Tsvangirai, Tendai

Biti, etc..., everyone else who is against the ZANU-PF hegemony to get under one umbrella. *I have now included Biti because as I have noted in previous updates to these essays he has left the MDC now and has created his own party, to add to the many splinters of the MDC. As I have argued above this is untenable. We don't need more of these one personality parties. We need all these opposition parties to unite into one force.*

There is no sense for the Western countries to think side-lining Tsvangirai and splitting the opposition would deliver the goods. This robot controlling of the opposition by Western nations, especially Britain and the donors has to stop. These Western nations should know it's not about how much they think a leader is suitable or unsuitable to lead this party but about the general people's view, because, ultimately, it's us who would vote, with or without their monies and support. Wealthy businessman George Soros, the British ambassador in Zimbabwe, and the president of Botswana Ian Khama (according to the *Sunday Mail* of 9 March 2014) have been some of the robot-controllers of the MDC who have been quoted as to have called for the MDC leader to vacate his position because he has failed. The question is to whom, in Zimbabwe, the likes of Soros and Khama have talked to, in the MDC grassroots, who told them they want Tsvangirai out. This is a misguided attempt, appropriately known by Mugabe as *regime change agenda*, which they are trying to effect in the MDC. These Western nations should know that the ZANU-PF now controls most of the rural Matabeleland because of the breakdown of the MDC of 2005. The MDC-N faction that had the majority seats in the Matabeleland now doesn't have anything, and the MDC-T only has Bulawayo seats, and that as the MDC has broken again, along Tsvangirai and Biti lines, these are just going to fragment the two provinces they still have most seats in; Harare and Bulawayo, and the ZANU-PF would swoop in on both, and will ultimately win the last fortress against the ZANU-PF's hegemony in Zimbabwe.

It was even misguided, on the part of the Western nations (European Union members, Britain and Sweden), in the 2008 election to support different opposition leaders, Simba Makoni and Tsvangirai. The 8% plus vote Makoni got in the March election in 2008, if just half of it, which may have been from people who had been duped to vote for Makoni because of their dislike of Tsvangirai, could have voted for Tsvangirai or not vote for anyone at all, it could have pushed Tsvangirai to beyond 51%, enough to land us into holy grail. Yet, Sweden with its monies felt it was necessary to sacrifice us our freedoms, just for the Makoni and the 8% project. We couldn't still be trying to figure out how to remove Mugabe from power now. Multi-party democracy in Africa is different from Europe, the Western world need to be told. The way to go is to band in, in one camp for the opposition first until they have achieved, and then we will try to develop and look for more alternatives, only after breaking down the ruling party's grip on power. They should check with how Zambia achieved on multiparty democracy. It only happened when the Zambians had broken the grip of UNIP by banding around Fredrick Chiluba's Movement for Multiparty Democracy. And even in huge democratic countries like the United States, Britain, France, it has been pretty-much two parties democracies. It's funny that Sweden thought they should be more in a baby democracy like Zimbabwe. But now, at the least, these Western nations should be working behind the scenes to unite all these parties, by refusing their dope monies to any opposition leader who thinks he can have it his own way.

I don't simply buy into the theory that these opposition parties can't be made to work together. They have come from the same oven, and share pretty-much the same ideologies. That they are at each other's throat is because of their coveting of donor money and stupid egos. They know they cannot stand divided, going forward, but as a united front. If the ZANU-PF can be able to make the late greats, Edison Zvobgo and Simon

Muzenda in the touted old Masvingo factions' games stay and work together in the ZANU-PF, and if they can be able to make Joyce Mujuru and Mnangagwa still work together, for the better of the ZANU-PF party, why not these opposition leaders?

Looking across Zimbabwe's populations, in and outside the country, and trying to find someone whom the country can unite around, as a possible force to dethrone the ZANU-PF from power is like looking for a needle in a bucketful of mealy meal. It's safe to say there is no one I can think of, off my head. Other than the usual little supported alternatives to Tsvangirai, the likes of Welshman Ncube, Ndumiso Ndabengwa, Simba Makoni, and the latest additions, Tendai Biti and Lovemore Madhuku. There is no one else with the political will to come head-on with the formidable ZANU-PF. They have been suggestions of the likes of business moguls like Strive Masiyiwa, Mutumwa Mawere, Herbert Makamba, who are great business personalities. Of course, there is huge respect for Masiyiwa, in and outside the country, but he simply is not a politician, but a businessman. The same applies for the other two. The politics of Zimbabwe is not about the technocrats or the learned but of power-clout politicians. And for someone to come up in this over-contested and fragmented opposition grouping and curve a niche it is difficult.

I also think Zimbabweans do not easily take to new politicians. You need to be inside for some time, fighting the system, creating the followers slowly until you have a base. Morgan Tsvangirai came from a long way-off in the ZCTU fighting the system such that when he and the MDC project decided on being a political party they had great following already because of mostly the work they did with the ZCTU. That's why I feel there is no one outside those who are already politicians by their own right who can really pull people, a lot of people toward their cause and come head on with the formidable ZANU-PF.

I need to clarify something here. I am not saying there are no other people qualified to be the president of Zimbabwe other those already fighting for it. Hell no, I have never thought that job is very difficult to do. Anyone with a bit of education can do that in any country in the world. But for one to get there they have to come head-on with the system that might make or break them. That's where a lot of us will fail. A pointer is on Mutambara who was drafted pre-2008 elections as a possible replacement of Tsvangirai, who has faltered. So, I don't see these other alternatives creating anything better than what the likes of Simba Makoni etc..., have been able to do. They have the money, but it's not money that's needed now. It's a recognisable and forceful leader in the opposition we want.

Zimbabwe is too much polarised into these two camps (ZANU-PF and MDC), or on the two personalities (Mugabe and Tsvangirai) to the level of creating cults along those lines. So that's why I think these two camps still have a huge advantage against any other opponent toward winning any election in Zimbabwe. So that in the meanwhile it has to be someone who is already in the trench who would have to deliver us to multi-party democracy.

It makes me go back to the MDC. It is our only way out of this quagmire if we were to unite around the MDC again, and trying to fight the ZANU-PF as a united front. We might disagree on who in the MDC should take us to Holy Grail, but it should be under the MDC banner. Here, let's not think of the most perfect entity but the most workable. We are still in the trenches, so we need to be flexible, and keep in sight of the ultimate goal. The MDC has very important structures into the grassroots, national following and consensus, and can easily get back the international respect and backing it had. None of the other opposition parties or new alternatives would have enough time to make any dent into the ZANU-PF.

It has to start with all these smaller opposition leaders, this move towards conglomerating around one opposition party. They should realise they cannot deliver on their own, and seek engagement with the larger opposition party, the MDC-T. They should engage the MDC-T with their egos safely tacked inside, and not to demand for positions that the MDC-T might not have or be willing to give up. And, those in the MDC-T should be open to these smaller opposition leaders, giving up some positions to these. All these small opposition parties should at least be allowed to join major decision making bodies of the new MDC, like the National decision making bodies, so that their influence in the organisation becomes effective immediately. It's stupid and naive for the opposition MDC to think they could lose people like Ncube, Coltart, Sikala, Priscilla Misihayirambwi-Mushonga, and still want to continue losing some more through the ensuing disagreements, and hope to fight the ZANU-PF, who still have all its leaders, baring those few who left and or died, since independence. MDC wouldn't have any chance without this alignment and re-organization. This is the most favourable dispensation that could have a huge chance to fight the ZANU-PF entrenched hegemony.

Chapter 10

Post-Election Zimbabwe's Economic, Social, and Political Landscape

I had a date with someone, so I took the trouble to dress up, a bit. I wanted to take her to see the dam, Seke-Harava Dam, in Hunyani River. I had been to the dam, a couple of weeks before taking photos, and I found I liked seeing it, and thought I could bring her to this dam. Water is as closer as one gets to perfection on finding a rendezvous with a date, especially if it's your first time going out. So, as I got to the fringes of my street, I saw all the young man of my street sitting in the gulley besides the road. It was pretty much everyone I knew who was there, and it was on Tuesday, midweek.

"Hello guys...I can see every headman is here...what's the event", I asked them as I shook hands with one by one.

Zvicha said, "Go and tell Mugabe what you saw. Tell him to visit Svosve Street."

At first it wasn't clear what he meant, but I later understood.

Fanuel helped me, "When you get into town, please tell him that you saw everyone in the street."

He thought I was off to town, and my namesake, Tendai, said, "He should know that we don't have anything else to do with our lives, but litter the streets, and just talk nothing."

At first I said, "I think he knows", and then I retracted.

"I don't think he gives a damn."

"NO", Callistus, a university graduate, failing to get a job for 5 years now, said.

I am not off to town; I am just going down some couple of streets. I knew even if I were going to town, I would never be able to say what I had seen to Mugabe. He lived in his ivory tower, at State House, and nobody litters the streets around his place, with despondent people. I wouldn't even come closer to his gates, to start with, so I had no way to pass these young men's messages. I left them as I went to my date, but when I had just left them, I told myself,

"Maybe, I could tell Mugabe what I saw today, maybe someday he would read my work and if I were to write about this, maybe he could know."

And I knew that was the only way for me, but I also told myself, "If he doesn't really know what is happening!"

I knew he knew what was going on in the country. He had professed, time and again, that he loved us that he was prepared to die for us.

Is he really prepared to die for this country?

Why is it that we have never seen him in the streets, seeing what is really happening. My former general manager, at AMTEC motors, a certain Joel Mapurisa, told me that the best managers, in a company, go down into the shop floor, and see for themselves what was really happening, rather than waiting for reports, which might be written to protect the leader and the report writers. Why is it that I never heard, all through the thirty plus years we have had Mugabe as our leader, that one day Mugabe just decided to visit some street in Mabvuku, Chitungwiza, Mbare, Mpopoma, Rujeko, etc., just to really get an idea of what was really happening. Why does he profess to love us to the extent of dying for us when he doesn't care to come into the streets where we battle everyday to stay alive and fight the war with us?

This is what we are now doing everyday, battle for our breath, otherwise we are getting to a point where we will let go and go back to the chaos of pre-2008. We are on the edge again, as things tighten. I have been talking to people, since the 31 July election which the ZANU-PF swept, by getting two thirds majority, about our chances.

A month after the elections things began to tighten with a lot of companies that had been waiting for a chance in change of government, closing off. The industrialist left, so did a lot of people who had come back, thinking we were on our right path to sanity, recovery and development, with the GNU entity. With ZANU-PF's absolute majority, a lot of people realised that they had no chance in this situation, so they are leaving in droves, again. Those who have the wherewithal are leaving, and day by day, we count the numbers. Day by day the companies are closing up, and relocating, some back to South Africa, some abandoning their industrial properties altogether as they leave for outside of Africa. If you were to go to the industrial area, it is a cork, an empty cork. There are very few companies that are functioning, barely functioning, with bare workforce. Companies have been lying off workers and streamlining their operations, and most have stopped hiring new workers.

It has been the government that has been the last employer for some time, but this year, the military is not recruiting. It is using what it has inside its ranks to fill in cadet positions. That's another pointer of the things to come. The other government jobs that are a rage with everyone is the teaching, nursing, and police professions. These are the jobs that seem available to every young person who enters the job market. I know of people who have Masters Degrees who have resorted to teaching primary school kids as temporary teachers. I know of accountants who have become teachers, marketers who litter the streets with no jobs, business graduates who are now lecturers at professional colleges. Considering that the country has plus 13 universities that are brimming with new students, I wonder where these thousands of graduates are going to be finding the jobs, after completion of their courses, when companies are downsizing. I wonder where the thousands who would come out from the colleges, all over the country, would find the jobs to work. I wonder where the hundreds of thousands who would graduate from both "O" and "A" level would find the jobs. It's an incredible situation we are in.

The agriculture sector is dead. It is simply political to hear someone saying we are growing in this field, in this sector. If you were to travel throughout the country during the rainy season, you would realise we are nowhere near growing. We are on our knees. Millions of hectares are unused, by the new farmers who were resultant to the land invasion of year 2000. Between 2000 and 2002, some 11 million hectares were confiscated from 4000 white farmers and redistributed to an estimated 127,000 small-farm families and 7200 black commercial farmers, and these farms remained unutilised, 15 years down the line. Those who are struggling to do something on these farms are producing very little to account for much to the GDP of the economy. We used to be in the top 6 in tobacco farming, which was our biggest agricultural foreign currency earner, but we have plummeted down. I am told by insiders that even tobacco companies in Zimbabwe do not use the tobacco we are growing because it is of low quality. They would rather import tobacco from Brazil, at $3/kg, than buying the low quality tobacco from these new farmers which is going for $4/kg. This insider told me that these new farmers don't even know how to grade the tobacco, such that quality and junk tobacco is put in the same pack, thus the pack is generally below quality standards. Even the process of growing the leaf is not professional thus it produces low quality tobacco. Most of these farmers are complaining that even the price of $4/kg is low, and that they can't pay back the loans they took to produce it, pushing them off these farms. We are now 15 years since the forceful takeover of the farms by the government in 2000, and I believe if this programme was working, and had been done the right way, we should be starting to benefit from it, but it is still malfunctioning.

The people who got the farms were not really trained to run these, and most were just political people who wanted to benefit, getting a place to build homes on. They didn't take these farms because they really wanted to make a difference, to change their destiny, and the country's destiny. If they wanted to do something beneficial to the country they should now be producing. Most of the A1 farmers were given less than 10 hectares, which I feel they should be maximally using now. If you calculate that the farmer would develop a hectare every year, they should now have started using all their land, by about year 2010, in spite of any other problems, but most still plough a couple or so hectares and the rest is left unused. And those who got bigger hectares, the A2 farmers, should now be utilising half of these, at least that. These A2 farmers had the advantages of getting inputs from the government, for many years now, and with this help they should be functioning commercially. It's now inexcusable for these new farmers to continue complaining about financial incapability. It's inconceivable that they think the country should keep subsidising them inputs, and produce nothing at the end of the season. It's high time the country should start demanding, from these farmers, that they either produce in their farms or leave the farms. This idea of creating perpetual dependences, in every aspect of the country's development and social aspect, isn't getting us anywhere.

If I am staying in the streets, anywhere in the country, and do not get anything to subsidise my living expenses from the government, but still the government get my taxes in several aspects economically, like job taxing, sales tax I pay when I buy things anywhere in Zimbabwe, tax from the payments of shelter, water, electricity etc... Then these farmers should start paying up for these grants they get from the government, as well. Otherwise they should leave the farms and allow those who have the love of farming at heart to takeover. It's time to depoliticise the farming issue in Zimbabwe and reverse it back to be an economic aspect of the country. The unfortunate thing with this unplanned land reform was there were no checks and balances put in the whole programme, not even monitoring.

One of the checks that should have been made as part of the contract with these farms, as a social contract of some sort, was people would only stay in those farms if they were utilising them productively. The government should have instituted mechanisms that would allow them to monitor progress on these farms, so that those who were not improving their productions, despite the help they were getting from the government, should have lost their farms by now. If we all know that the land belongs to all of us. Yes, that these farms are mine, just like they are for these new farmers, or that of white man dispossessed from the farms, then we should have the right to demand that they leave these farms if they don't produce. These farmers didn't buy these farms; neither did the government from the commercial farmers, so it is the country's land. The country should be able to take it back from non-producers.

The way to go now in these farming communities is for this probe to happen, and those who are not producing to leave the farms, and come and stay with us here and scrounge for an existence just like everyone else is doing. We start employing people into these farms who love farming. We do away with this colour issue that has beclouded our judgements over the years. If they are still some commercial white farmers who want land, they should get the land. We can still break down the amount of hectares we give to one person so that everyone who wants to get back to the farms will get an opportunity. If there are black farmers who have been maximally using their farms, for the benefit of the country, they should be left alone, and be helped to continue producing. This is the most important resource we can all be able to exploit easily, to get a lifeline out of it, than any other ones that require high capital input. The idea is for us to find employment for a lot of us who don't have anything to do. If the thousands of graduates who are going to come out from our educational system fail to get a job in the industries and mines, then they could go back to the farms and start producing, otherwise these people, I am afraid, won't have anything to do, by the way things are turning out in Zimbabwe. They are simply no jobs for anyone, let alone for those just coming from the colleges and universities. We can't even export this talent because there are a few places for them out there they could get jobs in. Most other countries in the Southern Africa have unemployment rates that are growing. So we are going to have to figure out how to employ each other here. And agriculture is one such way we could start creating jobs.

Going back, on the education system, that is producing these hundreds of thousands of graduates every year, I feel it is not the best it ought to (can) be. Since they changed from Cambridge examination to local Zimbabwe School Examination Council examinations, it has gone down. There are several years when the marking of the exam papers, for both "A" and "O' level exams, was in shambles to the extent of having them marked by people who were not qualified to mark these papers because those who were qualified had refused to mark the papers, due to their poor working conditions and pay issues. They were allegations that the 2007-2008 papers were marked by the soldiers. Since they turned to local examinations, the exams papers have been leaked pretty much every year. There is not enough security to make sure the papers are not leaked. In one instance, the minister of education then, Edmund Garwe's daughter, was found with the paper, and this resulted in the resignation of the said minister.

Another important aspect related to the examination is that students in Zimbabwe are just concentrating on mastering the examination techniques, and the past papers, such that there is little foray into acquiring the knowledge about any subject to be examined. It has been adopted as the culture by teachers who do not want to waste their time in teaching students to acquire broader knowledge of the subject, because it would eat into their time, time they could use in doing paid extra-lessons. It's so easy to gauge this; talk to any student, be it in primary or secondary, or even high school, about the general stuff, or general knowledge in the subjects they are covering; they have little knowledge of this stuff. You can't even have an informed discussion with these students because they simply do not know stuff that they ought to know, as well. What we are creating with this type of education system is Robotic Education. This is the kind of education system that doesn't develop students' analytical, intellectual, creative, synthesis and intuitive abilities (a traffic robot doesn't have these abilities, doesn't check the traffic, it is programmed to action) but is just focussed on passing the exams papers by cramming (almost programming) the answers. So, these students' analytical, creative, synthesis, intellectual, and intuitive abilities are very poor. *Chunghea Oliver* in *There is No Cholera in Zimbabwe*, in her essay, BLACK AND BLUE: A FAULTY EDUCATION, talking of the Korean situation seemed to be talking about Zimbabwe now,

> After finishing classes for the day, students are highly recommended to participate in self-study until 9 to 10 at night. When this is over, many of them go to cram schools to supplement their study. The cram school industry is a powerhouse. It is energised by a vision common among parents, the wish for a more competitive son or daughter, and which charges top dollar for access to additional teachers and materials, the hope for that extra edge to get into the right school. The sight of masses of young uniformed students walking around late at night with backpacks stuffed with books is staggering for visitors arriving for the first time in Korea.... These are not the

110

only problems. Test-driven standardised education seemed to weaken students' ability to think critically and take ownership of their learning. As students are heavily directed to focus on textbook contents in order to prepare for standardised tests, they spend all their energy on memorising information as much as possible. Instead of developing creativity, problem-solving skills, and higher order thinking skills such as analysis, synthesis, and evaluation, students are forced to drill the facts into their head until they remember (2013: 201).

Another problem, in our poor education system, is that there is this all-encompassing focus on scientific, mathematical and to some extent, business subjects, and all the other subjects are given less importance. I asked my grade seven nephew what he knows about art. He said they stopped doing anything arty in their grade 3, and he described a bit about it, and basically, it was crafts he knew of. Even in secondary education there are very few, former class-A schools, who have art subjects, and nothing at "A" level for pretty much every school in Zimbabwe. There are no craft schools. There are no sport schools, real focus on sport in the schools, other than the usual schools sports. PE (physical education) is only done in early primary school years, and after that, there is nothing done much to develop talent in sporting activities. Its only sports that are easier to manage and nurture that are worked on, for example, soccer. It's getting to such a point that it is the only sport that every young kid could dream of, because it's the easiest for every kid to try it out. A kid only needs a ball made of plastics, and any sort of ground, or open space. The other high paying sports like cricket, rugby, tennis etc..., are inaccessible for a lot of the kids, and are only available at better schools because these schools can afford the expenses involved in developing and acculturating these sports into schools.

There are very few practical subjects done in schools, as well. Mostly, it has been a bit Agriculture here, building there and Metal work here, for the lot of the schools. And other subjects like Technical Drawing, Fashion and Fabrics, Fabrication and Machinery, etc..., are not covered throughout the schools. Even those that do practical subjects, the focus is not on developing these students such that when they graduate they could do these for a living. It's about passing the subjects so that they would add up on the number of subjects passed. So that, with this concentration we have been having on science, business and mathematical subjects, we are producing students who mostly, and as I have argued above, would fail to get jobs in these science and mathematical business fields, and due to lack of jobs, would know little else to do with their lives. They don't know any other skills because they haven't been given the opportunity to explore anything else other than these subjects.

We are a country that in the past has prided itself for being the best on the continent, in terms of education and literacy rate, but we are now producing an inferior type of education, even though we might still be ranking high in terms of literacy rate on the continent. We are producing educated fools, people who think theirs is to be workers, not inventors or employers, people who wait for directives, people who just follow the trend, and people who are just interested in jobs. That's why if there is a field in Zimbabwe that has shortage, for instance in the 90s; accounting, legal fields, doctors, teachers... had shortages back then, and everyone who graduated tried to go for those fields, with the result that in a decade these fields were flooded.

Now, with the migration of skills that happened during our troubled years (2000-2009), in which fields like teaching, nursing, doctors lost a lot of workers, these fields are now the rage with every student because there are certain jobs and security, as well. Fields that used to shine like marketing and accounting, etc..., are flooded and very few now are choosing these fields because they know they wouldn't find employment after graduation. Instead of the country focussing in developing other skills, like art, crafts, sporting, and technical fields, so that students would have a wealth of possibilities to choose from, the focus is on science and mathematical business fields.

The only art college I know of in Zimbabwe is the *Zimbabwe College of Music.* Universities cover scant fields in this vast field, as well. I don't know of any university, and we have plus 13 universities, that offers a creative writing degree. As a writer I was forced to develop myself, yet the field employs people and is very important in the development of the country and literacy. Despite this, Zimbabwe has consistently produced some of the finest writers to ever grace the continent. I am not saying we don't need these scientific mathematical graduates, but we should try to create a balance whereby we produce what we can absorb. We are not a developed economy and such other fields like agriculture, crafts, art, etc... could help us in developing our country. It's no secret that without good investments in the agriculture and vocational skills sectors our economy would die.

We should think small, and start focussing on small scale work practices and crafts like what the Japanese did after the Second World War to grow our economies. We can only do that by focussing on vocational skills development, and small crafts and skills like carpentry, building, metal fabrication, pottery, art, sculpture, agriculture etc... If we were to focus on these fields we could grow our economy. It's important for us to give a great focus on the agriculture and community endeavours as well, and that's why I have argued we need the farms to start producing.

Agriculture is the future of the world economies, by the predictions coming from the experts now. It is agriculture that will become important again, as the world suffers from shortages caused by global warming effects, which is creating dry spells throughout the world. Rather than the world fighting over fuel, it would be fighting over food. If we can focus our skills sets in this field, devise and adopt better farming practices that harness good environmental practices, we will develop well. Countries like Brazil have now started benefiting from adopting better agricultural practices, and it has grown immensely in the last few years and now makes the top 10 economies in the world.

We have, generally, all-year round good weather and temperatures that allows for any type of crop to be grown, at any time. We have sunny days almost 365 days per year. We have great agricultural land. We have generally good rains every year. We have the right mixes to make agriculture to develop us. We made a huge error by taking the farms chaotically and we have paid the consequences of such a decision. As I argued in the last non-fiction book on the same issue, in the essay, FARM INVASION EPISODE, in ZIMBABWE: THE BLAME GAME (Tendai R Mwanaka, 2013), we made a wrong decision in the way we implemented the land reform. But, it's now time to move past that and figure out how to right the mistakes we made. We have the land; whether black or white, let's now use it, period!

Another aspect of the country that is in the sorrow state is in our workplaces, both public and private, due to the mismanagement and corruption. Corruption has been rife in our country since we got independent, and as I argued in the essay, DOING MUGABE, in, ZIMBABWE: THE BLAME GAME (Tendai R Mwanaka, 2013), this corruption was acculturated by our government, and permeated every level of the society. Even with the GNU entity, it never died, but embroiled even the MDC into it, through massive corruption that happened in the councils that it controlled. As I write this piece, for a couple of months now, they have been corruption exposures that have been making headlines in Zimbabwe. With

114

the council leaders of Harare being said to be earning in excess of $US20 000 per month, and Cuthbert Dube, at the insurance company he works for, is said to be netting over $US200 000 per month, not to talk of what he is earning at ZIFA where he is the boss. It has been exposed that most of the senior managers of companies and government departments are earning salaries that rivals their counterparts in developed countries. It's obvious these salaries are unsustainable because we are in a dying economy, with most companies barely working.

For the $200 000 that Cuthbert Dube is getting in a month, he is gobbling enough money that could pay for hundreds of the company's workers. For a company that employs, let's say 50-100 workers, especially most parastatal divisions in Zimbabwe. The senior managers or directors are paid upwards of 20 000 per month. With the same amount they can pay upwards of 40 workers with one senior manager's salary. It is obvious Zimbabwe is a tale of two countries, with the senior managers and directors owning their own Zimbabwe, building beautiful houses in the ever expanding northern suburbs of Harare, and the rest of the country renting or lodging rooms and houses in the southern and western suburbs of this city, striving every day to stay alive.

It's the poor workers and the unemployed who have been made to deal with the real effects of the country's meltdown, with teachers and other public servants getting peanuts when their bosses in the government get well paid. The problem is that these poorly paid workers can't go on strike anymore because they would rather keep their jobs than to totally stay at home. They know the country is brimming full with people who are qualified to do the same jobs, and their employers can ill-afford to fire them and replace them straight away. So, you would rather work, than go on strike. For some years now, I haven't heard of any public servant, let alone private workers on strike in Zimbabwe. They just can't afford it. This has resulted in the massive exploitation of the workers in Zimbabwe, with companies like SINO-ZIMBABWE being accused of using colonial methods, of beating workers for workers to increase production. The total effect of such a situation is that we have a workforce that is barely putting a meal on table. And it is even an incredible impossibility for those who don't work at all.

Those who do not work have resorted to unofficial trading. The country is made up of traders and sellers of commodities. Things that used to be rubble, and were an eyesore, like old metals, tires or dumped cars are now big business. There are traders who ply the streets, everyday, looking for these metals, which they would use in their metal works. Dumped cars are being exhumed, and beat into shape and be fixed for the road. In every street you could count several road tables that have been converted into convenient shopping points. People can just put four bricks into a square, and cover these with a flattened cardboard to create these open tables, on top of which convenient foods are displayed for the buyers, stuff like sweets, airtime cards, chips, bubble-gum, popcorn, snacks, bread, sugar, candles, matches, school books, music CDs and all sort of traditional fruits. Not to talk of several thousands who ply the streets throughout the day selling stuff, and those who have flea market tables that sell clothes, shoes, bags etc. Zimbabwe is now a selling market, especially for South African producers. Since very little comes from our industries, thus the people are forced to enter the selling field rather than the production fields. It simply is important for the people to find something to do with their lives, for someone to figure out what to sell to survive, but the problem with this unregulated trading is that the government isn't getting anything, in terms of taxes, let alone the local authorities.

This also applies to small companies that are still employing people throughout the country. Most of these small informal companies are unregistered such that government

116

doesn't collect taxes. The only place the government is getting taxes from is in the formal industry, which is small and dying. We have a government, due to its mismanagement and corruption, which has made its own job impossible to do because there is not enough money in its coffers.

The same is happening in every facet of industry, even the mining sector where there is good growth for the past 5 years. Most of the companies that are exploiting these resources are unregistered, so are thousands of illegal miners. These do not pay taxes to the government, and mostly their produce is not sold in formal trade routes, with a lot of smuggling of the minerals to outside the country, to countries like South Africa. These would ultimately benefit South Africa, rather than the country they have been extracted.

During the GNU entity there was a furore when it was exposed by the finance minister, Tendai Biti that even in legalised mining, like the diamond mining in the Marange area, the money was not being channelled into the right department or ministry, the revenue department ZIMRA and Reserve Bank of Zimbabwe. These were both under the minister of finance, Tendai Biti, of the MDC. They have been unconfirmed accusations that a lot of the diamond is being smuggled outside the country by bigwigs in the ZANU-PF and defence departments in connivance with Chinese miners, which have not been benefiting the country. The total effect of all these malpractices is that it is killing the industry and the government. In making the two dysfunctional we are making the whole country dysfunctional, and renormalisation of the economy and country has hit another hard rock, in fact it is getting worse and worse. Since the 31 July election there has been a downward trend in growth, and capacity level of companies have gone below 30 % as of 1 January 2014 from around 50% in the GNU entity, and upwards of 75 companies have ceased doing business, and this has happened in just half a year since the elections. By the time we are through the next five years to the next election we might be in inflationary times like yesteryears'. Money has become difficult to get and cash flow is constrained and very tight. The minister of finance has officially accepted that the country is now in a depression.

A lot of companies haven't been paying their workers for some time now. With councils like Chitungwiza city council, and parastatals like former ZISCO STEEL, now hitting on a year without paying for their workers. There are also a lot of companies that have ceased producing anything, and barely open their companies, with unpaid workers, just hoping things will improve. With the failure of companies to pay their workers; and it's usually shop-floor workers who are not being paid, for their managers and senior workers are paid; this has resulted in the flow of money throughout the system stagnating and creating cash flow problems throughout the system, and ultimately cutbacks in consumptions and purchasing. The cash shortage problems also stems from the fact that most of the money is in a few hands, with the bloated salaries I noted above that senior managers are earning, so that it is not circulating. These people are holding onto the money and the economy is now retracting. The biggest reason we have this cash flow problem is because we don't produce much anymore to create foreign currency inflows, but rather we lose the little we have in reserves by importing everything we need for day to day living. So we have been net exporter of foreign currency. The other reason is we don't attract much in terms of direct investments into the economy anymore, and foreign governments' grants have since dried, too.

It only requires one stupid bungling, by the government, and then we will be back in inflationary times of the 2000s, especially if they misguidedly change the currency to the Zimbabwean dollar note. We are still using the US dollar, and this has been keeping things stable, but tight. If the situation continues being tight the way it has been since the elections, the government is sure to do away with the US dollar because they can't devalue it, or print more money to deal with the liquid crunch. Once we adopt a fluctuating currency, like the Zimbabwean dollar, then we are sure to hit the inflationary trends again, because this same government is known for mismanagement of the currency in the last decade, that resulted in hyperinflation. This is imminent especially when we still have the same undisciplined government which I still blame for necessitating the hyperinflation of the 2000s, which they fuelled by printing, mostly unnecessary money, to deal with any crunch.

The country's roads, bridges have fallen, for some years and, have not been serviced. The water and electricity, as you can deduce from the diaries from ITS NOT ABOUT ME, and the story, TUESDAY, have not been available, with water being only available for some couple of hours one day per week. The councils barely carter off the bins, or service anything due to lack of funds. Everything has gone down, some things are non-existent now, for some people, due to lack of funds and development. I have been hearing the current minister of finance, Patrick Chinamasa saying we can fix our things on our own and grow without Western support. It's easy to dispute him and ask him what they have done for 15 years now. Yes, it can happen. It has happened in several countries all over the world. We did it, as well, during the UDI period in the sixties and seventies, and we grew our economy, despite sanctions from much of the Western world. We can still do it. But it's just talk shop for the likes of Chinamasa to say that. He should support his verbal comments with actual action towards that. He barely was able to create a budget this year, long after the deadline of November, and worse still; the budget doesn't have any formula you can decipher towards finding solutions to our problems.

The government, as usual, has developed another economic development programme to add to the tens of those which it has implemented before, ZIM-ASSET. It's not usually that they are not well thought out programmes, it's just that implementation has always been Zimbabwe's Achilles heel. We simply do not have people who are dedicated enough to implement these tens of programmes. Sometimes the programmes are farfetched and too ambitious, top to bottom programmes or on the surface programmes that do not burrow into the people in the streets or target the ordinary person in Nyanga, Muzarabani, Gokwe, Bubi etc. Until we start focussing on the people who really need these programmes to work to change their lifestyle, we are always the losers from these programmes. The problem is most of these programmes are created by top people in the country, and focuses emphasis on enriching these same top people.

I will give a few examples, the land reform program benefited the top people in army and government, and the indigenisation law being implemented in the companies has benefited those who have money already. I don't see how these two programmes have helped the majority of Zimbabweans so far. It's just self-serving grab and run economic programmes that would ultimately affect the entire majority for the worse. The farm invasion as we have seen didn't benefit the entire country, only a few top people, and the entire country were affected by this programme for the worse, so has been this indigenisation programme. No company is willing to come and invest in Zimbabwe now, with the result that it would forfeit its 51% stake to locals, thus with non-investment in our economy due this law and the resulting closures of companies by those being targeted for seizure through this law, a lot of people can't find employment, and thus a lot of people have become poorer.

So, it is time for the likes of Patrick Chinamasa and his colleagues in the government to start focussing on important things that would grow our economy rather than spouting political bile. I want to see him making it work without complaining about sanction this and sanction that. It's not the whole world that has applied sanctions on Zimbabwe. We can work with those who are our friends and do away with the Western. This ZIM-ASSET programme needs to be pushed into people in Nyanga, Uzumba-Maramba-Pfungwe, Mutoko, Matopos, Lupane etc..., and start functioning there. He should put all the resources into this drive, and work from the field, not from his spacious offices in Harare for us to start developing as a country. And as I have argued above, the focus should be on agriculture and small vocational skills. These will employ the people and earn a livelihood for the entire country,

Mugabe, since the eighties, nineties, the last decade and now has been saying it is the agricultural sector that is important and has tried every year to try to help people in this sector to plant their fields and achieve in their endeavours. I believe he has been correct in this understanding, but why is it that we have failed. He blames the entire country for failing him. That's where I don't agree with him. As a Zimbabwean I can only be against him during the elections period and try to vote for someone else because deep down I know he has failed me, but once he is in the government he is now my president, whether I like him or not. That means I will try by all means to do my best to help him in his vision of the country. It's his party and cabinet that has failed him and us, not me, an individual who is trying to survive. Its people in his government right down to the district level who have failed him and us. To me it's him who has failed me.

He is the CEO of Zimbabwe, so he is to blame for non-performance of this company, Zimbabwe. It's him who creates cabinet to help him. It's him who appoints pretty much every government worker. It's him who employs that teacher who doesn't teach our kids well. So it's him who is to blame for the non-performance of the agricultural sector. Most of the cabinet ministers he still has in his cabinet he started with these since independence in 1980, 34 years ago, and he has shuffled these over the years and added a little new blood. If they are the same people who have been failing him, why has he kept them?

There is some time, in the 90s up to early 2000s, when he experimented with technocratic teams that comprised Simba Makoni, Bernard Chidzero, Christopher Ushewokunze, Abednego Moyo, etc., and those cabinets created a lot of vibe, and were growing the country well. But, it was still the political element in him and the ZANU-PF that made these technocrats fail to do their jobs well. He would go against their sane and balanced decisions, especially Simba Makoni and the industry minister, Abednego Moyo, who argued against the government paying the war veterans those billions that depleted our coffers in the late 1990s, and many other economy-destroying strategies of Mugabe, such that Makoni and Moyo left government. If he can't trust his ministers who want to do their jobs well, and trust those who want to use uncouth practises against economic development, it's him who is to blame when these methods do not work. He went against Herbert Murerwa, in the mid-2000s, and took Gideon Gono's advice of dealing with the economic problems. These measures created and fuelled hyper-inflation on the country and precipitated the meltdown of the economy. So, he has no one to blame but himself. He should now learn from the economic ministries in the GNU that the MDC controlled. MDC had relatively young ministers and leaders and these like Biti, and Mangoma in particular at the energy ministry made their ministries shining beacons and righted the economies. Before Mangoma, at the energy ministry, we had very acute electricity cuts but now it is relative. He introduced prepaid meters, florescence lighting in homes, such that a lot of electricity that was being wasted was saved and the cuts are now stable. Instead of Mugabe crying pell-mell over the landscape blaming others, he should start from home and right in his office, and start employing the right people for the right jobs.

Chapter 11

Security Sector Reforms

It is estimated that Zimbabwe's security sector has caused the death of more than 40 000 people, 10 000 missing, and more than 300 000 internally displaced since independence in 1980. Peter Eden, 'Counting the Dead: Zimbabwe's Victims', *The Informer*, 22 October 2008.

These included those of the Gukurahundi in Matebeleland in the 1980s, and those from the post-2000 military operations. In this essay, I am focusing mostly on the military's exigencies of post-2000 when they really got involved in our democratic institutions and in the next essay on recommendations on how the security sector reform could be managed and done.

In his book, *The Case for Security Sector Reform in Zimbabwe*, Knox Chitiyo (2009: 3) who I would rely heavily on posit,

> From 2000 until the establishment of the GNU in 2009, politics in Zimbabwe was dominated by military exigencies. There were five major trends. First, by 2008, there was no real distinction between the party, the state and the government. Second, the formerly opaque politics/military/business nexus and 'covenant' became open and structured. Third, politicisation and political loyalty, rather than professionalism, became the guiding ethos within the security sector. Fourth, Zimbabwe's political economy, the 'strategic sector' and many state institutions were also militarised and politicised. Fifth, presidentialism was also institutionalised. It would be simplistic to characterise the security sector as militarily or politically homogenous– there have been serious problems regarding morale, politicisation and training – but the

combination of institutional esprit de corps, politicisation, patronage and proximity to power means that the security sector still remains broadly loyal to the ZANU-PF grouping within the GNU.

In, *Anatomy Of Political Predation* (2011: 6) Bratton and Masunungure feels it started straight off from independence, saying,

> While predatory tendencies were evident from the outset within the ruling party – especially with regard to the use of violence to "consume" political opponents – political leaders did not completely abandon a developmental agenda until confronted by a combination of pressures from international financial institutions, their own restive political base, and an emergent political opposition. From the late 1990s onward, however, the ruling coalition adopted a "laager" mentality in which the goals of state building and economic development were sacrificed at the altar of elite political survival. An increasingly narrow coalition of civilian and military leaders with roots in the country's liberation war violently clung to state power and turned the instruments of coercion toward managing sham elections and looting the country's wealth.

Our security sector has been involved in many military operations against its civilians since 2000, some of which are:

Operation *Tsuro*. This involved approximately 1,500 war veterans, 1,000 soldiers of the 5th Brigade (these are the same soldiers whose heavy handed tactics in the Matabeleland had caused the death over 20 000 civilians in the 1980s), 300 CIO operatives, approximately 200 members of the police, and 5-6,000 ZANU-PF volunteers, including ZANU-PF youth members. It was like traditionally when we would go into the bushes to hunt for *Tsuro* (Hare). There are all sorts of traditional weaponry like rods, machetes, pangas, axes, etc..., and there are no rules here. Anything that can kill our *Tsuro* is allowed to be of use. This was the idea they took to when they invaded the white commercial farms, with the intention to kill or push out these *Tsuros*. A *Tsuro* in traditional folklore was the cleverest, conniving, fastest animal, so the whites were likened to this animal. Operation *Tsuro* had three objectives, which included forcibly taking over the farms of the 1,600 white commercial farmers, and intimidating and using violence against known or suspected opposition supporters to ensure that they voted for the ruling party. By the time Operation *Tsuro* ended, it was estimated that 700 farmers had been driven off their land, 135 opposition members had been killed, and dozens more traumatised by violence.

The 2002 presidential elections were also run as a military operation. A national command centre was established, initially at the Sheraton Hotel, but later relocated to Manyame Air Base. The strategy involved the military taking command of the electoral institutions; the tactics included the use or threat of force to ensure voting compliance. The Electoral Supervisory Commission was staffed with retired and serving officers, with Colonel (Rtd) Sobusa Gula-Ndebele appointed as head for the duration of the elections. Two of the six members were army staff, and the management of the electoral process was run as a military operation.

The third major operation was Operation *Murambatsvina* (Drive out rubbish), which followed the parliamentary elections of 2005. During a three-week operation in May-June 2005, police and army units used bulldozers to demolish hundreds of shacks and houses in high-density urban areas nationwide. It directly displaced over 700 000 people, and indirectly displaced over 2.4 million people, and had far reaching economic, political, economic effects on the rest of the country. For more information on this operation check online, Anna Tibaijuka's drafted UN report, on this clean-up and the resulting refugee crisis it created in Zimbabwe.

The fourth major operation was Operation *Makavhotera Papi?* ('Who did you vote for?'). This operation involved a combined forces military assault on the rural areas, particularly in Masvingo, Mashonaland, and Manicaland Provinces. These were former ZANU-PF strongholds that were punished for voting for the MDC in the March elections. The operation was prepared by the military but involved the police, CIO, war veterans and the dreaded 'Green Bomber' youth militias. Schools were turned into military headquarters, and the provinces became 'operational zones'. People had limbs cut off, were beaten, and were killed for voting for the opposition. People were forced to go to rallies, attend night vigils (pungwes), indoctrination camps etc. The country became a warlords controlled zones with the police as silent spectators and sometimes instigators. Senior army staff coordinated the strategy, the aim being to terrorize people into voting for ZANU-PF in the June run-off election, or to force long-time MDC supporters to flee the area and thus lose the chance to vote (voters can only do so in their registered ward).

In late 2008, the security sector launched a series of paramilitary attacks against illegal gold and diamond panniers. Operation *Chikorozha Chapera* ('No more mining') involved the police and army in coordinated attacks against legal and illegal gold panniers. Thousands were injured and an estimated over 200 were the fatalities. And a follow up Operation *Hakudzokwi* ('No return') was later launched against the 30,000 diamond panniers still in the Chiadzwa diamond fields in the Marange area of eastern Zimbabwe.

The Zimbabwe Defence Forces have also been involved in two major external conflicts since 1980: Mozambique and the Democratic Republic of the Congo.

Smaller operations have included Operation *Taguta/Sisuthi* ('We have eaten') in November 2005; Operation *Garikai* ('Live well'); and Operation *Dzikisai Madhishi* ('Remove your dishes'). Operation *Taguta* was an attempt to create a command agriculture system reminiscent in some ways of the Bolshevik *prodrazvyorstka* agricultural requisitions of the 1920s. Small- to medium-scale plot holders, who normally planted a variety of cash crops, were ordered to plant only maize. In some areas, particularly in Matabeleland, other crops such as sweet potatoes and ground nuts were ploughed over by the army. The traditional crop cycle was severely disrupted, leading to increased food insecurity and the threat of starvation in more remote areas. The Joint Operations Command (JOC) was the dominant force in Zimbabwe for the better part of a decade. The JOC, which operated at grand strategic level, was the successor to the tactical-level Rhodesian JOC. Bratton and Masunungure (2011: 26) note that,

By the early-2000s, a Joint Operations Command (JOC) of security agencies had side-lined the civilian Cabinet as the supreme, but unofficial, decision-making body in the party-state. The JOC originated in the colonial era as a counter-insurgency coordination organ chaired by the army commander. Now it was convened on a rotating basis by the heads of the army, police, air force, intelligence service and prisons, the JOC reported directly to the President. It took on any policy issue deemed to impinge on national security, broadly defined, and has inflected the management of the party-state with military-style "operations." Without prior warning and with little advance planning, the regime suddenly announces "Operation X" or "Operation Y" for implementation by army, police or armed auxiliaries.

Generally, these are some of the operations that our security sector has been involved in, mostly against the wishes of its electorate. Even the wars we were involved in, both DRC and Mozambique, the majority citizens didn't approve of these forays, and the DRC war depleted our foreign reserves and ushered in our financial problems and the meltdown of the economy.

These security sector forces – army, air force, police, intelligence and prisons – reports to the President. The intelligence unit (CIO) is given funding from the President's office, the costs of which do not appear fully in the finance minister's annual budget. The most powerful arm is the Central Intelligence Organisation (CIO) whose operatives have infiltrated government ministries, NGOs and political parties (including the two MDC formations). Prior to the transition, top leaders of the defence forces vowed publicly not to recognize Prime Minister Tsvangirai in any official capacity. Some security chiefs – the Commander of the Zimbabwe Defence Forces, the Commissioner-General of Police, and the Commissioner of Prisons – still refuse to salute him. These holdouts from the old order have also declined to attend milestone events in the life of the transitional government, including the inauguration ceremony for the Prime Minister and official gatherings to launch the *Short-Term Economic Recovery Program* and *100-Day Plan*. Thus, Zimbabwe's transitional government inherited a deeply politicised security establishment whose loyalty to elected civilian leaders is in open doubt.

The dreaded and most pervasive C.I.O (Central Intelligence Organisation) is estimated to have approximately 10 000 personnel, however it is pervasive such that it has many more auxiliary and informal staff in its rank. There is a point when people thought it employs just about everyone who is for the ZANU-PF, because it penetrates into every organisation, company, and institution in Zimbabwe such that it's difficult to know who is or who is not. This is the most involved in Zimbabwe's culture of violence, and the most feared by its citizens.

The second security sector organisation is the Zimbabwe Defence Forces (ZDF), which has strategic power within the military-political nexus. The ZDF is embedded within the CIO, police and prisons, all of which have been thoroughly militarised, both in outlook and methodology. The ZDF comprises the Zimbabwe National Army (approximately 30,000 serving personnel) and the Air Force of Zimbabwe (approximately 5,000 personnel). The ZDF is configured for a 'two war' capacity (internal and external, and conventional and counter-insurgency warfare).

The Zimbabwe Republic Police (ZRP), together with the war veterans, has become the day-to-day enforcer of state security. The police have had to adopt an increasingly wide remit from 2000. They have continued to cover their traditional mandate of anti-crime policing, but the militarisation and politicisation of the police has resulted in their deployment in paramilitary operations as part of the JOC. This is another very influential of the security sector organisation because it deals with the day to day running of the country and has been variously used to suppress protest or any meeting deemed to be against the ZANU-PF, to the detriment of its tax payers, the people. All security sector experts agree it is this sector that requires more immediate and comprehensive reforms to make it professional again. There are currently approximately 25,000 serving police personnel.

The Zimbabwe Prison Service (ZPS) numbers approximately 5,000 staff. Contrary to the popular belief that the ZPS is constituted as a civilian organisation, the ZPS mandate explicitly states that 'the ZPS is a uniformed paramilitary organisation under the Ministry of Justice, Legal and Paramilitary Affairs'. Though it is not directly involved in the open abuse of citizens, but many a prisoner has died in its overcrowded, food shortage, bad conditions prisons that look like concentration camps. Learnmore Jongwe, a former MDC National Organising Secretary was killed in dubious circumstances in these prisons, and many others. There are non-politically motivated deaths in this organisation's prisons, too, due to the conditions, not to mention many abuses including sexual abuses or sodomising by fellow prisoners or officials. There are forty-two main prisons nationwide with a holding capacity of 18,000, though there is disagreement over how many prisoners are held in Zimbabwe's cells. The ZPS has stated that there are currently 12,971 prisoners, but unofficial sources have put the figures at nearer 30,000.

The Zimbabwe National Liberation War Veterans Association (ZNLWVA) and the Youth Brigades are the main militia groups, and are arguably the most highly politicised groups within the security community. These two groups were the 'shock troops' for the farm invasions, assaults on farm labourers, and attacks on the opposition, particularly in the rural areas and small towns. The war veterans number about 30,000, with an estimated 10-15,000 on call for military 'operations' at any given time. The Youth Brigades, who came to be known – and feared – as the 'Green Bombers', number approximately 15,000.

There are also opposition forces of both MDC groups, and the MDC-T in particular has internal security departments. These are manned by former security sector personnel, and are designed mainly to protect party officials, staff and MDC supporters. There are also youth leagues, which are used to counter those of the ZANU-PF.

Although not formally part of the JOC and the security sector, part of Zimbabwe's judiciary has become an auxiliary of the security sector. From 2000, the state led what former High Court judge Benjamin Paradza called a 'systematic government crusade to purge the judiciary'.

In total, there are over 130 000 personnel in the formal security sector organisations, most of which have been used to systematically abuse the citizens. Our entire security sector is geared towards internal dissent, rather than external, such that there have been overlapping of functions and job specifications, and through their leaders, the security establishment has protected and allowed each other to abuse the citizens, without recourse for the abused because of the politicisation of these organisations and the judiciary. Bratton and Masunungure (2011: 27) observe,

> Because shadowy militias act as proxies, it is often unclear exactly who is ordering abductions and torture and who is executing these orders. And even when abuses in police or intelligence services are documented, perpetrators are rarely charged and invariably escape penalty. Ordinary Zimbabweans have been traumatised by such developments. Public opinion research shows that more than four out of five citizens fear to speak openly about politics. Political fear has in turn led people to adopt a risk-averse approach to public life: in contrast to the 1990s, citizens now manifest unwillingness to organise resistance, for example by joining strikes or protests.

These security sector leaders, through JOC, has been unofficially running the country with a hostage president and it is imperative, for the normalisation of Zimbabwe that there are security sector reforms whereby some senior security sector leaders who have been partisan should resign or be re-educated on and about their actual mandates.

The security sector reforms have not been able to accrue any progress, in the talks in the GNU, with the president categorically saying it was not up for discussions, reneging on the commitments his party made in the GNU negotiations, to do these security sector reforms. The following two areas, Knox Chitiyo (2009: 34), feel are pertinent in reforming the security sector:

SSR (security sector reforms) in Zimbabwe should have two main objectives:

~ Civilian-Military Covenant: This first goal of SSR would incorporate pragmatic processes to make the military part of a social covenant with the people.

~ Institutional Reform: This aims to refurbish the internal architecture and vision of the security sector in Zimbabwe so as to improve efficiency and morale.

There is consensus between some people in the opposition politics that the MDC has not been able to put pressure on Mugabe to make these reforms in the GNU. In his visit of the Western nations, Tsvangirai was vilified by his supporters who have alleged that Tsvangirai has been too soft in his dealings with Mugabe, and the security chiefs who continue to have civil society and MDC activists arrested and beaten. During his June 2009 tour of the US, UK and Europe, Tsvangirai was taken to task by Zimbabweans who questioned his judgment, in his dealings with ZANU-PF.

It was in our plebiscite that the battle ground of security reforms has been fought fiercely, because since the creation of the GNU, five MDC-T MPs have been arrested and imprisoned on various charges of corruption and fraud. Another eleven MDC MPs are facing charges. The arrests, and lengthy jail terms, fuel speculation that ZANU-PF's aim was to overturn the MDC's wafer-thin parliamentary majority (by law, if an MP is absent from the House of Assembly for more than six months, they automatically lose their seat). The arrests of MDC MPs also posed a serious challenge to Tsvangirai's leadership, as MDC supporters demanded that he confronted ZANU-PF and the Attorney General over this and other issues.

Chapter 12

Recommendations on Security Sector Reforms

In this essay, just as in the previous one, I will rely heavily on recommendations made by Knox Chitiyo in his book, *The Case for Security Sector Reform in Zimbabwe*. Chitiyo says the first port of call is to start instituting dialogue between the security sector and the citizens. The relationship between these two entities is built on distrust, fear, disdain. It is important for this dialogue to start happening, at whatever level.

I know it's easier to write it on paper like I have done, but for it to start accruing meaning, or even consideration by the players, it requires more than just saying it has to happen. The security sector chiefs need to have confidence in the system, or the talks, for them to open up their work for scrutiny, let alone for discussions towards solving issues they feel protect them, which impinge on the rights of the people. With an intention of allowing for this to happen, we have to encourage these security chiefs to open up for discussion by promising them immunity from prosecution or libel. Possible prosecution by the justice system is the most important reason why both sides mistrust each other. I would have wanted to have the security sector chiefs be punished for the crimes they have committed against the civilians but that won't help us going forward, anymore. But, they have to admit to the crimes they committed to allow for those they hurt to deal with their pain and hurts, and move on. We really need a truth and reconciliation on the level of the one done by the South African government in 1990s.

If it really needs to be pushed to beyond the liberation war to account for those who still have wounds and hurts inflicted during the independence war to find closure, let's do it. It should encompass those who were killed in the Gukurahundi atrocities in the 1980s, those killed and victimised in the post-2000 military operations and those whose rights are being infringed now. It has to be a holistic and altruistic process towards healing whereby every blade of grass has to be covered in normalising entities in this project known as Zimbabwe. We need to move forward now, but we can only do that if we are open to each other about the wrongs we have done to each other, otherwise we are creating a perpetual retrogressive cycle of people who are not normal people and a country, people who continuously infringes and kills each other for nihilistic reasons and nebulous patriotism and nationalism that's so vacuous.

Knox Chitiyo (2009: 37) also says,

> Although regional, continental and international practitioners and analysts should also input on the debates, the security sector and defence debate in Zimbabwe should be Zimbabwean-led." He goes further by proposing that we should create a National Defence and Security Strategy (NDSS). "There needs to be a National Defence and Security Strategy (NDSS), which draws a roadmap for Zimbabwe's current and future defence and security requirements.

These security sector reforms need to be wider, comprehensive and sequenced, whereby the process need to be carried over a long period of time. We don't have to solve everything once off, but to start small by bit small. Chitiyo posit, "There are eight entry points that can allow SSR to begin immediately in some areas; other SSR processes would have to be done over the medium to long term." (2009: 37)

The following are the short term security sector reforms he proposes:

Short-term SSR

Entry point 1: Regularise the National Security Council

Chitiyo proposes that we can use the March 2009 National Security Act which included ministers and security services chiefs from the original NSC, which managed the war economy for Zimbabwe between 2003-7, and ruled Zimbabwe as private fiefdom, but failed in reigning in the economic meltdown. The new NSC created in the act of 2009 was envisaged as a multiparty grouping that monitored the security of Zimbabwe. It included president Mugabe, vice presidents (Joseph Msika and Mujuru), prime minister Tsvangirai, deputy prime ministers (Thokozani Khupe, and Mutambara), Finance Minister Tendai Biti (MDC-T); Defence Minister Emmerson Mnangagwa (ZANU-PF); and the Home Affairs Ministers Kembo Mohadi and Giles Mutsekwa. The security sector chiefs will also be ex-officio members of the NSC.

If security reforms had happened in the GNU, it is this grouping that should have pushed for it, but with the July 2013 election in which ZANU-PF is the sole party in the government, and has absolute majority in both houses, this arrangement might not work anymore now. Going by this entry route is now very difficult because the opposition doesn't have good and direct influence on the security sector chiefs they might have had when they were part of the GNU entity. It can only happen through the goodwill of the security sector chiefs and the ruling party's good faith, otherwise this entry route is difficult to use, so I might suggest we use the other entry routes. Chitiyo proposes,

Entry Point 2: Revisit the Defence Forces Commission

The Defence Forces Commission (DFC) deals mainly with internal administration and morale in the ZDF. The MDC and, perhaps more importantly, members of the armed forces have expressed a desire for the DFC to be more pro-active regarding morale and conditions of service within the military. The DFC needs to undertake a national consultation with the military to listen to grievances. (2009: 38)

We could use this by improving the conditions of our security sector members, and in that we might help in developing professionalism in the entire force. If the members are well paid and looked after there is little chance of them being used for selfish and self-fulfilling reasons by their bosses, thus they can assert professionalism on their own.

Entry Point 3: Overhaul the Electoral System

Although the last election was done before pending issues like the security sector reforms, ZEC reforms, media reforms, and electoral system reforms which hadn't been completed, it may be time for us, all Zimbabweans, to start the process towards these reforms. The electoral system in Zimbabwe is flawed. It's not just the Voters Roll that is in shambles.

In trying to rectify some of the problems of the last voters roll, in which it was found that over 1 million people who were dead were still on this voters roll, they also created some more new problems. In the last election, people were moved to places they have never stayed in their entire lifetimes. For an example, a brother-in-law of mine, who has been a voter in a his ward since the 1995 election, who has a residential property in this ward, who was registered in this ward, when he went to the polling station to cast his vote, his name was not anymore in this ward. He had been transferred to another constituent, in Harare. He had to travel to Hatfield to cast his vote. Some people had their names transferred to places that would have taken them an entire day to reach, to cast their vote.

Another problem of the voters roll is even the voters roll wasn't available for inspection before the election. We couldn't check whether our names were still there in the voters roll, so if you were unlucky to have your name transferred to a faraway place, you wouldn't cast your vote. The other issue to do with the electoral system is on our legal system whereby if there is an election dispute, it has to be dealt with by the same partisan justice system. The MDC had to partition the court to force ZEC to release a voters roll before the election, but despite winning the motion in the high court they couldn't get the manual voters roll, which the ZEC said wasn't printed, and let alone, they couldn't get the electronic copy, only after the election. The ZEC refused with an electronic voters roll, as they said it had many technical problems, but it is this that was important for any reconciliation to happen because it contained the latest information on the actual number of voters for particular wards and the entire country.

Even the election result partition had to be withdrawn by the MDC when they were instructed that in their arguments or witnesses they were not allowed to call the ZEC, Registrar general etc... for questioning or as witnesses. But, it was these same people who were heading these bodies that had made a mess of the whole electoral system, but they were said to be immune against any kind of deposition, let alone for criminal charges. This issue of electoral laws has to be dealt with for Zimbabwe to ever have a free and fair election. I think the voters roll they are using has to simply be disbanded, as they disbanded the Rhodesian voters roll after the 1985 election that favoured the whites, and we will start a fresh process to register our names, in a new voters roll. This voter's roll is just a fraud, so also are the electoral laws. Another related issue is when the electoral laws of a country deny its people not staying in its borders the right to cast their vote. There are people (in excess of 4 million), who stays just across the borders in Botswana, South Africa, Zambia, Mozambique who were denied their right to choose the direction and destiny of their country. The foreign vote should simply have been allowed. For us to continue using these flawed systems is a big injustice and insult to the Zimbabweans. We have some of the best legal minds in Africa and it's a shame we still have these stupid laws and systems in place. Chitiyo (2009: 38) observes, "Civil society

137

groups have made suggestions regarding the electoral review process. These suggestions include:"

• The Zimbabwe Electoral Commission should re-educate and be made professional again and efforts should be made that its neutrality is guaranteed.

• The judiciary should undergo reforms too, to make sure that it upholds the law in a non-partisan manner.

• The composition of Parliament should reflect democratic elections (meaning no one should be appointed to the parliament, only through by winning an election would someone becomes a member of parliament)

• There is a need for a comprehensive audit of electoral laws as I noted above, and in a number other essays in this book. Now, the problem is we are proposing a situation that might not be happening any time soon as the political will for this has changed with the new composition resultant of the July 2013 election. We can only apply pressure for these to happen through civil society, independent newspapers and the few opposition MPs that now constitute the new parliament. Chitiyo also feels it is also essential to take steps to ensure that elections are not politicised and militarised, ever. Here are the measures he proposes.

• We should create legislation that forbids military personnel (army, police, CIO, war veterans and youth militia) from the management of elections. In 2008, the military took charge of the entire process ('advising' voters on how to vote; commandeering the ballot boxes; and 'counting' the votes)

• We should provide for independent observers to observe when the military votes in various barracks across the country are being cast and counted. In 2008, soldiers and police reported that they themselves were under orders to vote for ZANU-PF and that their vote was not secret.

• We should allow international as well as regional and continental election monitors for local and national elections.

I still don't understand why the ZANU-PF and president are afraid of the entire international community's observers and monitors if they really have nothing to hide. If the president really wants to have an election that would be certified free and fair, he should open out his doors to those countries he thinks are against him. By having a free and fair election endorsed by these enemies of his, he would also win them over because they won't be any basis for them to continue punishing him.

Even at that, decisions to decide who to invite or not to invite shouldn't rests with parties or ministers but with independent bodies that are impartial and professional. Mugabe and his ministers and the party have conflict of interest in this decision because they are part of competitors. When they make these decisions they are being referees and players, at the same time.

• We should ensure that the ZEC – the traditional elections manager – is staffed by nonpartisan professionals and that it reports directly to parliament without interference from the military or other groups.

Entry point 4: The Prison Service

It is important to begin reform of the Zimbabwe prison system. Our prisons are overcrowded, dirty and lethal. Food shortages are common for both warders and prisoners, and what little food there is, is often vermin infested. There is also lack of enough blankets and protective clothing. On 31 March 2009, the South African Broadcasting Corporation aired its documentary on Zimbabwe's jails; the smuggled film footage showed stick-thin prisoners living in conditions reminiscent of the worst twentieth century concentration camps. The prison service is an easy and natural entry point because it bridges the security and justice sectors.

Chitiyo proposes five steps which could be taken immediately. These include:

• ZACRO (Zimbabwe Association for Crime Prevention and Rehabilitation of the Offender) should be encouraged to present an updated version of its 2008 report on the state of Zimbabwe's prisons to Parliament. With the justice minister and prisons commissioner-general invited to respond to find a way to implement these recommendations.

• A parliamentary committee should be established to investigate/audit Zimbabwe's prison system. This committee could be assisted in its work by the UN and by local organisations already in the field. A report should be compiled and budgets estimates made, that include.

• Following the SABC video report, the UN was allowed to deliver food, clothes, blankets, medication and medical care to some of the prisons. This needs to be regularized. The ZPS, in collaboration with independent organisations, should submit a budget of requirements (food, salaries, medicines etc...) This should be continuing beyond the GNU entity so that prisons are not death houses for prisoners.

• Budgets should cater for vehicles to transport suspects to court; there are only four trucks (often out of service) to transport prisoners from the three major prisons (Chikurubi, Khami and Hwahwa), as well as numerous smaller prisons. This means that in many instances prisoners' cases are not heard because they cannot appear in court. There are an estimated 7,000 prisoners in remand prison. Many have been there for years without their cases being heard; the lack of vehicles to transport them to court is one of the reasons for this. This is causing a lot of prisoners to serve terms for crimes they didn't even commit, when eventually they are found not guilty, yet they would have stayed in remand prisons for years. Even for those who really have crimes they committed, it is still an injustice to serve a term without being convicted. It's just as good to say our system assumes every prisoner guilty until proven innocent.

• A general amnesty for minor offences would clear the backlog. The yearly presidential pardons might be pushed into quarterly pardons or should cover a lot more prisoners to easy off the overcrowding and scarce resources of the prisons.

Entry Point 5: The Zimbabwe Republic Police

Most SSR prioritises the army; SSR in Zimbabwe should prioritise the police. This is not to downplay the requirement for SSR in the military, but the ZRP occupy the legal as well as the military and paramilitary domains, and thus have much greater daily interaction with the public than do the other security institutions. Reforming the police is a long-term project but certain things can be done relatively quickly. Chitiyo (2009: 40) proposes the following immediately:

• Acquiring vital equipment such as up to date computers, and patrol vehicles

• Improving basic training, and emphasizing human rights and respect for the law. This is already taught in police courses, but these fundamental values can never be overemphasized

• Instituting an anti-torture policy (criminal suspects and political prisoners are routinely tortured). There is too much torture in our prison system with some prisoners tortured to death before their trials happen. These torture tactics by the prison system are tantamount to infringement of prisoner's basic and fundamental rights and flies in the face of our justice system. It's as if once you become a prisoner you are no longer a citizen of the country, not even a person.

• Encouraging better civilian-police relations through improved community policing

• Upholding the Police Code of Conduct which already exists.

Longer-term reforms could include the reorganisation and retraining of public order units, such as the riot police; and ensuring that crowd control does not entail the use of lethal force against civilians.

Entry Point 6: Education and Civil-Military Relations: the Return of 'Big History'?

The security sector runs a variety of high-quality vocational and professional courses up to post-graduate studies. We should encourage civilians to take these courses; to create interactions between the civilians and military, thus breaking down barriers. Course content should also be expanded to include democratic discourses. The teaching of history at all levels should also be broadened to take a pluralist history perspective, the big history that includes multiple narratives that encompass everyone, not just ZANU-PF's point of view. The demonization of the MDC, Rhodesians, the West by the ZANU-PF, and the reverse demonization of the ZANU-PF by the West, MDC and Rhodesians should be a thing of the past. Let's just change the stories here.

In practical terms, we should entwine national educational revival with increasing and improving educational opportunities, curricula and teaching for the security sectors, this would be beneficial. All these security sector forces comes from the country's education system, so we could use this entry to institute better educational curricula and practices to our students in our schools and ultimately those who would enter the security sector fields.

Entry Point 7: Reconciliation

As occurred in 1980, the new government has stated its commitment to promoting nation-building through reconciliation. The GNU has created a National Organ on Healing and Reconciliation, which includes ministers from all three GNU parties. But with the new dispensation after 31 July 2013 elections we can only put pressure for reconciliation to happened from the outside now. The organ has since disbanded. But it is dangerous for us to ignore this just because we seem past the moment. This will come back and bite us, as happened with the liberation war, Gukurahundi atrocities etc. We should keep this in focus. As argued in the previous essay, SECURITY SECTOR REFORMS, let's broaden this national reconciliation to encompass those who suffered in the liberation war, in the Gukurahundi, and those of the post-2000 election period.

Entry point 8: Truth and Reconciliation Commission

Zimbabwe needs a Truth and Reconciliation Commission (TRC). The Zimbabwean TRC could function along the same lines as the South African TRC or the recent Liberian TRC; in other words, it would be an evidentiary rather than punitive body. The TRC would help to ascertain not just who the perpetrators were, but also who gave the orders, and the likelihood of new campaigns of violence. Chitiyo (2009: 40-41) goes further and observes,

A TRC would also be a site of cultural cleansing; in African culture, it is often believed that the victim of a violent death returns as a *ngozi* (vengeful spirit) to torment the living. Only when the truth about the assailant is revealed can the *ngozi* rest.

Medium- to Long-term SSR

Some process or reforms of the security sector have to be done on a medium to long term basis, for example for the police and army, for it is not easy to penetrate these security sector strongholds. Militaries are known to protect their turfs, even in huge democratic countries like the USA, especially against civilians.

"As ever, political will and the assent of the military is a pre-requisite for reform" (Chitiyo 2009: 41). Chitiyo suggests, and proposes the following ways in which we could do short to long term security sector reforms

Review National Security Strategy and National Defence Policy

Zimbabwe's national security strategy needs to be reviewed to ensure public consultation. State security shouldn't be dominant but human security. This citizen-centred concept of national security would in turn inform national defence policy (in other words, threat assessments, defence requirements, capabilities and budgets). Our ZDF should be prised-off the civilians and be refocused towards external missions, particularly national sovereignty, peacekeeping etc., where the military has a stellar record with UN, African Union and SADC forces. Each sector should perform its allotted tasks. The police would return to their role as civilian guardians of public order and the law. The size and funding for each sector would then be based on these recalibrated mandates.

Create a Defence and Security Commission

A Defence and Security Commission (DSC) could review defence and security in Zimbabwe, recommend reforms and point the way to a revised National Security Act.

Commission a Report on Defence and Security

The report would need to assess the strengths and weaknesses of current defence and security in Zimbabwe and outline the shape of Zimbabwe's future defence policy. As was the case with South Africa's 1996 *White Paper on Defence in a Democracy*, it should be about confidence building for Zimbabwe's citizens and the wider international community. Chitiyo (2009) proposes these issues which the report could examine include:

National Security

Zimbabwe needs a national security vision that is people centred not state centred.

Democracy and the Military

Democratic provisions of the national constitution and the military's own service regulations should be aligned. The report should make commendations on how this could be done, respecting both the military and democratic provisions.

Military Professionalism

Assessment of the levels of professionalism within the security sector and recommendations on areas where there are major weaknesses.

Depoliticisation

The levels and types of politicisation within the security sector, as well as in the public service, would be examined, and recommendations made as to ways in which the military could be depoliticized.

Role and Functions

The report would need to issue clear guidelines on the role and limits of the military in a democracy. This includes two aspects: the first covers role definitions of the specific military institutions, including the ZDF (army and air force), the ZRP, the CIO and the ZRP. The second involves presenting recommendations for specific security sector legislation which formalises the rule of law, and promotes democratic accountability within the security services.

Disarmament, Demobilisation and Reintegration of Militia Groups

Technically the militias are not standing armies, so a different type of demobilisation is required. The report should suggest incentives for disarmament, demobilisation and reintegration and ways in which this could be handled, particularly in the case of the war veterans and the Youth Brigades (Green Bombers).

Parliament and the Security Sector

The report would assess the relationship between parliament and the military. Emphasis should be made that the Military is answerable to the country through the parliament.

Education and Training

Zimbabwe has a strong tradition of education in the military. The Army and Police Staff Colleges already run highly rated courses in military and legal affairs. The report could emphasize areas in these courses that need expansions or re-thought to make the courses serve the country best.

Security Sector Budgets

The report would make recommendations on how greater transparency for security sector budgets can be achieved. Areas where cutbacks can be made should also be identified.

Right-sizing

Zimbabwe needs a military commensurate with its resources and needs. The report would evaluate what the size of the security sector should be. How many personnel (military and civilian) are required? Is the sector too large? We should also take into consideration the availability of resources. I think we have too big a military, considering we haven't been at war since the liberation there is no need for us to have that military that big.

Equipment and Control of Forces

The report would distinguish between security sector needs and wants with regard to military equipment. Given that Zimbabwe's security sector should, ideally, function as a democratic defence community, and one which provides human security to the citizenry, is there a requirement for state of the art light and heavy weaponry? Just as importantly, the report should detail the use of lethal weaponry and torture against civilians. It is important to ascertain what weapons were used, who issued them, and why.

Command and Control

The report would assess internal command and control structure in the security sector as well as between civil powers and the military.

Women and Security

In Zimbabwe, as elsewhere, women and children have not been spared from political violence and have often been specially targeted in some instances. Women have been raped, tortured, mutilated and killed, particularly during periods of electoral violence. Domestic and criminal violence against women is another, often interrelated, problem. Security reform proposals would need to be gender sensitive.

Militarisation of Elections

For the past decade, elections in Zimbabwe have been a catalyst for the military's usurpation of political process and for political violence. The electoral run-off of June 2008 is a case in point; more than 300 civilians were killed, with hundreds of others being forced to flee their homes. There would need to be specific recommendations as to how the military can be prised out of 'managing' elections. The role of international monitors is another issue which may need to be discussed in the report and in parliament. National elections in Zimbabwe, as in other countries around the globe, need international monitors if they are to be credible.

Transitional Justice and Reconciliation

The report would need to assess ways in which justice and reconciliation could complement security sector reform in Zimbabwe. Let's re-enact the organ of national healing and reconciliation post July 31 elections.

Empower the National Security Forum

Although the Defence and Security Commission would be the main enablers in the security discourse in Zimbabwe, there would also be an important role for a National Security Forum. Chitiyo (2009:44) suggest

> This would be an informal grouping of security practitioners, civil society, academics, and others – in other words all those with an interest in the outlines of Zimbabwe's restructured political landscape. The forum could be an 'ideas reservoir' which would complement, not compete with, the DSC.

I think we should expand that to include the whole of the country, not just specialist as suggested by Chitiyo. We are deciding the destiny of the whole country and there should always be respect of what the whole country thinks not just a few experts, so I suggest if this is to be done it should be focused on the whole country.

Enable Processes of Social/Informal SSR

Although the primary focus of SSR in Zimbabwe lies in reforming military culture, there should not be an obsession with a top-down, mechanistic process or output. Socially based SSR is very important, and is already happening in Zimbabwe. This includes school programs which raise awareness of the dangers of joining violent criminal and political gangs; and public awareness campaigns about security sector legislation (as part of constitutional awareness campaigns). Donor assistance from the regional and international community will be required. This can be state-to-state, or NGO-based funding. There are numerous organisations which have proven excellence and expertise in SSR; they range from smaller but highly effective African organisations, to state or regional organisations with a global reach. The issue with donor funding for SSR, as with donor aid in general, is not about who is doing the funding. The question is about whether indigenous people are partners, with equity, or whether they are merely recipients who are being used to service unrealistic targets set abroad, and/ or the profit margins of organisations. Donor aid, in the security sector in particular, needs to be *smart aid* which is based on realism, local needs and capacities; and most of all, common sense.

Chapter 13

It Stirs; It Stirs....And It Stirs

He has seen much more than he could even remember. With every new turn things changed. He has come to accept that there is no absolute in life, that life in itself is not an absolute, that there is always something stirring beyond the frontiers.

New things. New trends. New beliefs. New movements. New lives.... New, new, new, new... and everything becoming a terrifying make-believe frontier district, and always something beyond these new frontier districts, coming and changing considerably..., sometimes completely, what everyone has come to believe to as the truth. That man's life is a complete inexperience..., from the tot who has just entered an alien world, a world that adults call real..., to old age that is so innocent..., completely lacking, so uninitiated in new things that have come just lately, things that they never thought of, things that thinking about their existence seemed too farfetched an idea.

Today, Sekuru isn't so sure anymore. He isn't so sure whether he still believes in the exorability of the ultimate. He isn't so sure of the ultimatum entering into its own metamorphosis unending endlessness. There also seems to be too many casualties on the side-lines as if everything has derailed off the course. Everyone else, even those who wish to be side-lined were being swallowed unwillingly or held at deathly ransom.

There is also this feeling... A feeling of trailing behind, a feeling of being left behind in the hostile wilderness as things begin to gird-up faster and faster than he is able to keep abreast. There is a fast fiery wind in the air, even in people' movements, touches, looks, gestures and postures. It is a feeling of something stirring everything to a particular movement...

It is almost end of winter and Sekuru has wandered up to the fields. Something has compelled him to undertake this journey. A thought, a feeling, maybe something that pushes us and put us on invidious positions, positions that would allow us to observe things that not everyone else would be observing.

It has been months and months ever since he has taken this kind of a walk. All along he felt he was no longer capable of such a pilgrimage. But, somehow, he has managed it, almost as easily as if it is something he did regularly. He sits a little bit, under a 'burdened with fruits' Muhacha (Parinari curatellifolio) tree, just by the road's sides. He wants to rest his ageing bones and perhaps steal a glance at the wonderfully gentle, flowing veldts, which stretches from his feet until they glances the far-off Nyangombe River and the small patches of hills to the north.

Then, he sees a strange movement..., just a tiny blip of it. It is a very small, tiny insignificant movement. Maybe his old eyes are playing a cruel insane game with him or had he been expectantly waiting for this to happen. Such that he thought it happened yet in actual fact it hadn't occurred, maybe he is insane! It is that kind of sane insanity that goes hand in hand with senility. He really must be, now that he is so old he isn't so sure what actually tallies with serenity, or maybe...

Then, there it is, it's another tiny movement like the last tail of mist writhing out of the valley's banks under the sun's incessant pounding. It stirs; it stirs..., and it stirs... It is smoke from the burning fire started from the matchstick thrown onto the grass by the young man he has seen passing by. As the smoke starts growing, so does, in the first place, a tiny flame. It starts slowly, silently, slowly..., until it starts moving in the direction of the wind. There is something about this fire..., the way it started, its growth, and its suddenly faster and fiery movement... It is a fire that behoves a strong and strange purpose. He simply has to stir clear of it.

He takes hold of his walking stick and dashes swiftly like a young energetic man across the wide road to safety. And, he can't help musing about this magnificent spectacle; which was to find a lot of conquests in its brood, especially those that don't tune up to its prodigious movement, a movement that is intolerably too fast for the old man. It is not only this fire that makes him think about these dark sad thoughts. It is the merging panorama of warring feelings wrecking his old frame, agonisingly denying any defined form.

All the dry trees and even some green trees are burned. It burns tiny animals of the grass; ants, termites, locusts and some other bigger animals that it surrounds. Only those that can run faster and some many green trees survive from it but with visible scars to show. It speed eagles north and south along the road, thereby covering infinite-some distances in these directions. It stirs; it stirs..., and it stirs. It is now a body..., big..., insurmountable in its deadly quest to silence everything...

To change everything; to bring a completely new picture that has fewer or no linings with the old picture.

It stirs; it stirs..., and it stirs, again and again. Beyond the valley intersecting the veldt, beyond the upland, beyond the hills, in the far off distances the smoke and fire could be seen stirring higher and higher in dark-dusty clouds of smoke thereby reddening and greying the sky to the west.

It stirs; it stirs..., and it stirs, again and again. Small patches of smoke and sometimes fire, here and there doing their outmost to totally burn out the left over logs, dry cow dung, plastic papers and many other things that withstood the fire's first scotches which were now far of the horizon.

It stirs; it stirs..., and it stirs, again and again. For the first time that morning Sekuru feels the uneasiness evaporating..., leaving a feeling of loneliness, of being left behind..., unmoving..., in his own world.

It stirs; it stirs..., and it stirs, again and again. He starts crying silently. Big rolling tears tumbling..., one after another and another...

It stirs; it stirs..., and it stirs, again and again...

Chapter 14

Neo-Colonialism, Racialism and Imperialism: New forms of slavery towards a United States of Africa

"There is silver lining in every cloud", is an English expression I would start with in this essay. It means, there is goodness in every badness, or bad person, situation etc... There are two important, (as silver lining) presidents I would like to work with, especially about their beliefs over the issues I am going to articulate in this essay, president Robert Mugabe and the deceased former colonel, Gadaffi. My readers know that I have been a constant critic of the two leaders, and I still criticise them in a lot of their other policies.

Mugabe has stifled, killed, maimed any political dissent against his rule since liberation, in 1980, and has brazenly hung onto power against the wishes of his people. Gadaffi has done the same to his Libyan people, and has supported anyone who was against the western nations and ideologues, even people or groups who have expressed this disagreement through force, through wonton killings, which was deviant behaviour on his part. His deviant excesses were more felt by his own people, where it has come to light, in the hard hitting BBC documentary, that he raped hundreds or thousands of girls, beaten, killed, and maimed countless others. And, his deviant behaviour wasn't only with virgin girls, even boys whom he sodomised. Being overwhelmed in all this dark cloud, it is difficult to find the silver lining. The only one I could think of is his support of the sudden uniting of Africa into one country, which he shared with Mugabe.

I have respect for these two revolutionary leaders on this. They understood the western nations' tricks and machinations, of creating chaos in governance of African countries, for their capitalistic (big business) interests, and ultimately, its people. These Western nations have been creating wars all over the continent, and keeping us on each other's throats, rather than uniting us towards a course that would make us work together and grow our economies together, and uplifting our people. The latest western project is in Central African Republic (CAR) where France is supplying the rebels with war armour to fight the government in Bangui. South African soldiers who were helping the Bangui government had to evacuate out of the country as they were being slaughtered by these rebels, with French weaponry. The DRC has an unceasing warfare situation in its explosive eastern DRC, Sudan ended up getting broken into two, in a long running civil war, and the South Sudan is already embroiled in a war, less than two years after its creation, Mozambique's RENAMO is back in the bush, fighting the government with speculation that it is the Western nations that are fuelling all these wars.

I suppose, since South Africa has always supported the Western line on the continent, like the toppling of Gadaffi, which South Africa supported, it learned the hard lesson, that these Western nations are not really our friends. So far, it is easy for someone to think I am supporting the opposite, the Eastern nations, no. NO! The same intentions and self-serving attitudes of the Western nations have been embraced by the Eastern nations, like China and India, in the exploitation of African countries and their resources, without much benefit from these countries.

The Eastern nations are even bigger culprits here. They just exploit without giving much back, as compared with the Western nations. These countries soften their stance against African leaders (dictators) so as to keep friendship and trade with these African countries. They can develop, mostly, substandard roads, one or two in return; especially roads that lead to the places they are exploiting. In many of their companies, workers are treated like slaves, like for instance at SINO Zimbabwe, where it has been brought to light that workers were being hit by a whip if they were working slowly. These are practises that go back to colonialism that the Chinese are practising in Zimbabwe's industry, yet they milk our destiny recklessly. They would be doing the same thing the Western nations do saintly, that is, vesting their own interests. In helping the dictators who are no longer wanted by their electorate, to stay into governance through this support, they keep us bound to these dictators we no longer want, and ultimately keep us un-united, denying us our chance to create a united front.

Gadaffi and Mugabe were privy to these machinations of the Western nations. Even if their understanding was self-serving, in that they would preach to us that our Eastern friends were indeed good friends when they were not. The two were working tirelessly to unite Africa so that we would be one country. It was their vision, a vision that comes from our independence forefathers like Kwame Nkrumah, Julius Nyerere etc., yet some countries, like for instance South Africa, through its presidency (Thabo Mbeki), were for the gradual uniting of this continent, through first starting uniting through the regions and regional bodies like ECOWAS, COMESA, and SADC etc... Gadaffi was for the fast track African integration.

Uniting of Africa is our only way forward; it is our urgency of now. We need this, so with this in mind, I supported Gadaffi's stance. We simply need fast track integration into one union or country. The slow, drip-drip process of integration through integrating regions first can be torpedoed by these Western and Eastern nations. The biggest reason of sudden integration is it would present our exploiters (both Eastern and Western nations) with little space for them to get involved in small African countries' politics and governance, with the intention to destabilise and create chaos as they have been doing. United together, Africa would have enough political and economic clout to call out Western nations, but as small divided and poor countries we have no chance to stand up to these foreigners. The whole world would be forced to deal with one government in Africa, rather than the many that we are now dealing with.

The way we are now, we are made to compete against each other by these Western nations, like for example, Angola, Libya and Nigeria compete against each other, in trying to get a fair value for their oils, and usually they don't. Zimbabwe, South Africa, DRC and Botswana are made to compete against each other on diamonds, thus we are always getting a raw deal through this competition. Our resources are being taken for little gain to us, to build foreign economies. With the resources we have, we should now be the richest continent in the world since exploitation started in the previous two centuries, but we are still the poorest continent. Countries like Australia and Canada have used their vast resources to uplift their economies into the top 12 economies in the world.

With a united Africa, trade between ourselves was going to be the biggest push towards our development, than we would ever get from foreign trade. These Western nations and Eastern nations somehow know this so they work at polar, against each other, knowing that it would break us apart. The Western nations create pressure against recalcitrant leaders to its ideologues. They create wars, instabilities, and the Eastern nations would do the opposite, upending these dictators. In instances when the East wins, the resources exploitation is like a white colour war, and they would keep these countries in their fold by keeping a blind eye on governance issues. The West would ravage those that they can, exploiting them badly, too. We are left there in the middle with no workable alternative. In these endeavours, both the Eastern and Western nations practise a form of soft slavery, but more destructive than the old slavery articulated by old greats like Albert Camus.

I am saying a soft kind of slavery because it would seem it's not forced on us like the old slavery.

Lately, China, EU and the United States have created summits with African nations. They are usually disguised as summits to discuss on how to strengthen relationships between these nations and Africa, but there are forums in which each creates an open line with our leaders to necessitate exploitation of resources. For instance, the two Western nations, the EU and USA say there are interested in developing democracy on the continent, and the USA, through Barrack Obama's Washington fellowship for young African leaders programme, has created a scholarship, in which young African leaders are taken into the USA's educational and leadership institutions and trained to be better leaders so that they would come back to Africa and help improve democracy. They are exposed to these huge American institutions for a measly 8 weeks and they are supposed to be clothed with enough knowledge to change Africa. It is an ineffective endeavour. I haven't heard of what those who have been benefactors of this scholarship have done to develop democracy in Africa, or in Zimbabwe. If these nations are really interested in democracy in Africa they should invest on the ground, in Africa now, by creating the necessary and relevant institutions to safeguard and develop democracy on the continent.

There is still some African leaders who were not invited to attend this year, like Mugabe, and I wonder how America with its alienation of Mugabe at the Africa-USA summit are going to help Zimbabwe develop into a better democracy, especially this continuing alienation of Mugabe and Zimbabwe in most of these endeavours. The EU in its EU-ACP summit had excluded Mugabe, too. It was the support of fellow African leaders, when they told EU they won't be attending if Mugabe is still excluded, that the EU was forced to invite Mugabe. This is what we need on the continent, uniting together against any attempts to break us apart.

And, rather than focusing on young leaders, the USA should be focusing on those who are already in influential leadership positions because these are the ones who could have immediate effective change on democracy in Africa. These young people they are developing are going to be eaten up, excreted and or changed by the system. By the time they should be making changes here they would have adjusted to these undemocratic systems here, such that they would be our next oppressors and just as undemocratic. Most of these leaders who are undemocratic or who oppress their own people in Africa were trained in Western institutions, but are now killers of the move towards democratising of Africa.

China-Africa summit is just about business as usual. China is only interested in trade. Exploitative trading with African countries and on the other hand it offers friendship to these dictators so that they wouldn't be prosecuted for their crimes. I wonder why all these foreign nations are not making these summits to be about figuring a way to uniting the continent, so that we would have a chance to develop into a stable democracy rather, they are enslaving us with dictators, military juntas, undemocratic leaders, and corruptive leaders.

In, THE ANATOMY OF PREDATORS (2011: 46-47) Michael Bratton and Eldred Masunungure, arguing on leadership in Africa, and I am applying this to the above discussion on these summits to create relationship, leadership or democracy in Africa, posit:

> This last discussion brings us back to human agency. It is often said by casual observers of African politics that the continent needs better leaders. While there is a germ of truth to this insight, it places agency in the wrong place. Unless they are selfless public servants, political leaders are unlikely to voluntarily submit themselves to a rule of law, to strengthen formal political institutions, or to invest in economic growth rather than political patronage. In short,

democratic leaders rarely emerge of their own accord. They have to be held accountable by an active citizenry. And this is where democracy comes in.

This is where the focus should be on, on developing strong institutions and knowledgeable citizenship. It's the people who would create the good leaders.

The other slavery happens with the exploitation of our natural resources for little or nothing, as I have outline above. And the biggest form of slavery that is happening softly, which a lot of us don't seem to be seeing, is the taking of our brightest minds, our productive people into these Western nations. Most Western nations, if you were to go back to a couple of decades ago, were beginning to stagnant, due to their ageing populations. Eventually, if that trend was going to continue, it was going to result in negative growths. They understood this eventuality, so in the 90s (the now famously known, "decade of strife" by scholars), and the last decade, they created a lot of totally unnecessary wars, and instability situations, especially in countries that had a bright future like Iraq, Libya, Zimbabwe, the Balkans, in the middle east, in Latin America etc... For example economic crisis in Mexico, Singapore, Korea, Vietnam and the tiger nations, and in doing so, they destabilised these economies that had a glut of literate and rich populations, and a vibrant middle class.

These educated, the rich and middle class immigrated, mostly with their families, into the Western world. The reason why most Western nations are rainbow nations is because of this, and these new nationalities have enriched these Western nations. For destabilisation of Zimbabwe, for example, Britain benefited immensely with our over 1.5 million people, the most productive of our people, who now stay and work in the UK. Huge talents like Derrick Chisora (heavyweight boxer), Andy Flower (played in the English county cricket and later became cricket manager for the national team), Shingirai Shoniwa (lead singer of a popular British band, The Noissete) etc..., now benefit Britain than their originating country, Zimbabwe. Mostly, these people who left for the Western nations are young, working class, taxpaying, educated, 20-40 year old group who would go there and create wealth for these Western nations. These people are also coming from cultures where the family unit is a bit large (5 children average) family, and thereby, it is helping these Western nations in creating young, vibrant, race-less and innovative societies and economies, than what would have obtained with the ageing nations they had with their 2 children families and populations.

The inverse factor is it is continually weakening the developing countries because these are now just functioning as training grounds for the Western nations who would take all the promising minds into their fold. This is the largest slavery now happening, especially in Africa. The argument that these people they take will give back their wealth to the countries they came from doesn't have much value. It is still the same argument that the resources exploitation is paid for by the exploiters so we are gaining something in return. The truth is the best effect of the resource is felt in our exploiters' countries, just like the best effect of these migrant workers is felt in the countries they will be staying in.

Most of the money they get from their workplaces is spent in these Western nations, because they usually leave with their families, so their earnings are ploughed back into schools, healthcare, food, accommodation etc., for their young families, into these Western nations, thereby enriching these societies. We only get the leftovers for the work of grooming, training and advancement of these expatriates. As a simple example, check every Western nation's immigration and visa requirements. If you are skilled, if you're talented and intelligent, if you have your own money, you can easily get a visa, work permit, resident permit and citizenship in the Western countries. But, if you are a refugee and do not have a dime on you, you are blocked or harassed from seeking a visa or work permit, and in fact, you are a disease. These Western nations create these chaotic situations in our lands but only harvest the best, and leave the rubble. It's a refined form of slavery, but more devastating.

The unfortunate thing is we don't have leaders with gumption enough to take decisions towards the uniting of Africa. We need revolutionary leaders like the Mitterlands, Kohls, Adenuers of Africa for this project to hit great strides and happen in our lifetimes. The truth is the Western and Eastern nations do not want this to happen. Of course, they would tell us, with their words that they are for it, but their actions say a different story.

Here is where we are; we don't trust our leaders, we don't trust both the Western and Eastern friends, so for us to unite into one nation, it should now begin with us the people of Africa, on an individual to individual basis, not on the grand political level like what happened in Europe. The truth is our politicians are suspects as compared to their European equivalents I have noted above, so let's take it upon ourselves, and start the discussions, the movements, the talks, the impetus, and we will push our leaders to do this in our lifetimes.

I should start thinking of any other African country as a possible home for me. We share this same home together, not a home of colours. This is not a nationalist ideology. It's about the same soil and destiny home, baring the colours. I mean it doesn't matter one's colour, we are joined together by the soil we call Africa. Another way to make it happen is for us to move into each other's territories, and make it our homes. Let's marry (people and ideologies), let's fuse, and let's integrate on our own. Look at what is happening between Zimbabwe and South Africa, or just the entire Southern African region, even though most of it is not happening due to our free will, but the two people, Zimbabwe and South Africa, or the people of

Southern Africa are becoming one nation. We need that for us to move forward with this dream. It's not the leaders in the Southern Africa who are creating this infusion, it's the people, and the leaders are forced to implement rules to accommodate this phenomenon, to the benefit of us all.

The other slavery that is deeply ingrained in us; it is this that has been refusing us the chance to do this project, is the belief that we are not good enough as compared with the Western nations and their ideologies. We are made to be defined according to Western concepts and beliefs, as if these are waterproof. Thus we always develop negative concepts about ourselves. This negative perception of us goes down into tribal groups, language groups, cultural groups, countries, etc. We are made to think it's on the outside where we can find a way forward, thus we look to the Western nations as the light, and us as the darkness. But, the truth is we are our saviours. It's us who are our light and the outside is the darkness. We have to refuse this slavery for it is the most corrosive. It enchains us from trying to make strides towards our freedoms. If I am made to think a person from DRC as less important than a person in Europe to me, I don't just work with the DRC person, but the Western person. It comes from the Western nations' racialist and supremacist ideologies of yesteryear and, it still corrodes our psyche today. We need to focus or fight against this to be able to fight all the other slavery gimmicks I have outlined before, against our exploiters so that we will realise the ONE Africa project. Just this slavery alone will unbind our drive towards a United States of Africa.

Chapter 15

Towards Malemanialess In The Land Reform In South Africa

This essay follows my essay *Malemania* in *Zimbabwe: The Blame Game*, and in this essay we are trying to undo this Malemania disease in South African politics, so that we would get to malemanialess. As I noted this term, Malemania, was coined for a certain Julius Malema who works like and has views of a manic, who is now an opposition politician to the ANC, with his party, Economic Freedom Fighters. I am not worried of his many other views but it is on two views that we might have to undo him, appropriation of mines, and the land reform programme, and especially on the land reform issue.

According to *Africa Research Institute* document on land reform in South Africa entitled, WAITING FOR THE GREEN REVOLUTION: LAND REFORM IN SOUTH AFRICA (Online summary):

The 1994 pledge by the African National Congress (ANC) to transfer 30% of white-owned agricultural land to black farmers has been undermined by a lack of political will and financial commitment. Other policy priorities have taken precedence over land and agrarian reform. While millions of hectares have been transferred, acute poverty and unemployment are rife in rural areas.

SUMMARY
*Implementation of land reform is complicated by multiple objectives, and inadequate funding
*Food self-sufficiency equated with large-scale commercial farming, hampers agrarian reform

*Precarious tenure rights are symptomatic of wider economic and social inequalities

*Much redistributed land deemed no longer productive, with insufficient support for beneficiaries

*Potential of smallholders is under-exploited, rural unemployment at 52%

* Land reform is a significant political and economic opportunity for ANC.

The South African government has been accused of relegating this issue into indaba circles until recently with the growing popularity of Malema's views on this issue. In the April 2014 election Malema got slightly over 6% of the vote with his party three months old. He articulated this issue and it became the basis of his campaigns. This showing in the election by Malema has made the ANC to start to focus on the issue but it is still not on the centre of its important policies, due to the fact that the South African populations are predominantly urban (over 60%) and issues to do with land for this biggest chunk of the electorate are boundary issues. They are more concerned with food security in the farms and do not want disruptions in the farms, so that the ANC has been articulating more the concerns of this urban vote than the rural vote on this issue.

The slow pace has also resulted in high cost of land restitution. Both are attributed to the now abandoned willing seller, willing buyer (WSWB) principle. In the absence of compulsion, most landowners have been reluctant to sell to the state. Collusion between sellers, property evaluators and government officials – and instances of corruption – have inflated market prices. Furthermore, purchased land has been widely scattered and often unsuitable for beneficiaries. With even the latest review saying of the land distributed so far, 90 % is now unsuitable, thus the whole program has not been functioning well or being articulated well on South Africa's political landscape, until Malema came and made it the centre of debate in South Africa. This is definitely mirroring the Zimbabwean case and it should be a pointer of the future.

According to Malema and his party's views there has to be a land redistribution like the one witnessed in Zimbabwe, and mining appropriation like the one ongoing in Zimbabwe now, thus his party is for the economic emancipation of the majority blacks. Not really that! The problem is Malema doesn't know how to solve these issues as a party or as an individual. He always proposes the state should just take all land back and lease it out, for example, for 25 years. He has never thought out well on the mechanisms on how to do these reforms, effects of these reforms on both the industry and South African economy, plus whether the new farmers have capacity to turn that land to productivity. He feels like an opportunist who is raising these issues not to solve them but just to gain political and economic mileage out of them. And the danger is he is going to spur some not well-thought out alternatives to be pushed faster and be implemented, to the destruction of the industry.

One of these not well-thought out plans that has been mooted by the ANC will force commercial farmers to cede 50% of their farms to their workers. One can only speculate, but it is likely with this that the commercial farms will see large-scale disinvestment. Farm prices will collapse, forcing other farmers, who have used their land as collateral for loans, to also sell their properties. Movable assets will be sold to provide some capital for a new life in the city. Some also suggest we might expect more golf courses, light industry parks, gated communities and rural retirement villages, and conservation parks and holiday resorts as farmers shifted into other industries not affected by these policies.

It's the land situation in South Africa that this character Malema, through his homophobic views, is trying to rectify, that's a big problem for South Africa for me. We might try to just disdain his views because they borders too much on the leftist side. He simply wants the whites to surrender all the land or be pushed out and can do it in a chaotic way that the Zimbabweans did. That the land issue has to be redressed, I agree totally with him.

It was inconceivable for about 4 000 farmers to own the majority land in Zimbabwe before the forceful land reform; it is unacceptable for the minority whites (about 60 000 farmers) to own over 87% of South Africa's land now. Where I don't agree with Malema is on forcefully doing it. I don't also agree with the new policy to forcefully take 50% of land and give it to farm workers. But, it seems now too thin to understand that they might be that forceful taking of farms in the future but it will happen if nothing is done about it now. And as I blamed the whites in Zimbabwe for scuppering the government's efforts to acquire land before the forceful land reform, the blame should now be placed on the South African whites. Here are cold facts for them. Whether it is going to happen today or tomorrow, land reform has to simply happen in South Africa. It is better for these whites to gear towards this and initiate programmes where-by the process will start now. They could do what they did with the Black Economic Empowerment deals whereby the whites identified the black partners they wanted to accede a share of their companies to, and then help develop these blacks thereby accruing more wealth for both themselves and the blacks and also growing the economy without causing disruptions to the economy and country.

As more and more South Africans become aware of their poor backgrounds, and how these haven't changed much for the last 20 years South Africa has been independent, the more the majority poor will push their government to start focussing on them. The ANC might be saying now that there is going to be no land reform in the form of Zimbabwe's land reform, but as more and more people start questioning its delivery records, and the questioning has already started, and in the future election period, it is going to be forced to do this land reform to appease the growing majority of its doubters. This is the trend Zimbabwe went through since its independence, and it would be naive to think South Africa would avoid this path, considering also that there are no alternatives the ANC government is putting forward to the people. The South African economy has been contracting since 2008, and is growing very slowly and is not creating enough jobs for its people, so that the poor and unemployed have stayed poor.

A lot of South Africans still live in poverty ridden slam cities, and it is this lot that will question and force the ANC to find new ways of emancipating them. In the meanwhile the leadership and well-up people in the ANC are busy enriching themselves, buying farms, buying shares and equity in companies through the economic empowerment deals, and this lot is the one who have been hoodwinking the entire country and the whites saying no land reform in the form of Zimbabwe would ever happen, but they can do that for now for they are still working in little pressured political landscape. But, as long as Julius Malema continues preaching his gospel of land grab the more blacks are going to be convinced it's the only way to go.

The way to go towards malemanialess is for the whites to start this land reform earnestly, and start redistributing land, even to the blacks themselves without waiting for the government. I know they are few white people who would agree with this. They are still sitting pretty in their belief of the ANC's lies, that no land grab would ever happen in South Africa but they should be concerned that there are no alternatives for the blacks to work with. Pretty much the bulk of South Africa's economy is still in the hands of whites, and the majority blacks have little wherewithal, they should realise when push comes to shove the ANC would feed these whites to the angry blacks, for the piece of the slice of the economy than letting these same blacks remove it from power.

As long as we are in Africa the land issue is always taken as a political issue not an economic issue. Even the ANC had the land issue as one of the reasons it fought the apartheid system against for, so efforts have to be made now to sort this issue before it becomes too problematic for the country.

Chapter 16

The Strikes Years

I started working at T.E.J electric, an electrical installation company in mid-August 1997. We were installing electricity as a subcontractor on two sites in Harare under the LONHRO Construction Group, who were doing the major construction work. The two properties were Borrowdale Brooke houses and Heritage school which was in the Brooke area and the other one was the controversial mayor's residence in Gunhill, Borrowdale. The mayor's residence was where we were now concentrating on most of those days but once in a while we would go to heritage primary school to do final installation work.

Nobody liked going to the Brooke those days because it was out of the way, so far away from the city centre. There were no shops nearby. The mayor's residence was in an old suburb and near the shops at Newlands Shopping Centre, yet most of the Brooke had to be built. The time I spent working at the mayor's residence I got to know that the notorious dictator, Mengestu Haille Mariam stayed just nearby. There was also a notorious and partial to the ZANU-PF high court judge in the area, so that the area was well protected. It was Mengestu who interested me most. The road leading to his property was a cul-de-sac, blocked by the police and the area around was guarded twenty four hours a day. Such was the protection being afforded by us tax payers in Zimbabwe to one of the greatest perpetrators of human rights abuses in Africa. I felt sorry for the millions who were gassed by Mengestu in Ethiopia and Eritrea.

I have diverged a bit from the storyline. I want to talk of the strike days of 1997-1998, those halcyon students, Unions and the national strike years. Here is a graph of the strikes, please do note the increased number of strikes in the period 1997-98, that I am writing about.

Table 1: Strikes, Zimbabwe 1991-2000

	Jan	Feb	Mar	Apr	May	Jun	Jul	Aug	Sep	Oct	Nov	Dec	Total
1991												5	5
1992	1	2	2		1	3	1		1			3	14
1993	5	2	3	3	3		1		3	3			23
1994	2												2
1995	2	2	1	6	4	4	6	12	8	9	11		65
1996				12	9	6	8	3	4	13	7		62
1997	3	3	6	7	19	18	28	16	22	98	5	7	232
1998	6	9	21	9		20	3	3	16	10	5	17	119
1999	6	28	5	14	8	4	11	6	13	19	17	17	148
2000	5	12	14	8	16	12	10	22	10	9	12		130
Total	30	58	52	47	51	61	60	59	73	148	50	44	733

Source: Godfrey Kanyenze, "The Zimbabwean Economy, 1980-2003: A ZCTU Perspective" in Harold Barry (ed.), 2004, p.130. Based on statistics from Ministry of Public Service, Labour and Social Welfare, 2001.

There was this day when they called for this particular strike, the mother of all those strikes. That day I was working at the Heritage school. Information about the strike had been distributed late the previous day. Our management didn't subscribe to these strikes so they said we had to come to work. That day we came to work even though the other contractors at this construction site hadn't even pitched. Those that had pitched left early in the morning when they saw that the strike was ongoing. Our management said we had to stay a bit and see out to a bit of some work.

I was a general hand so I worked with an electrician and his name was Brian Makuwa. The time we arrived at the workplace was the time all the other construction companies were leaving, disbanding work for the day. So we stayed and worked a bit up to about ten in the morning, well thinking that there was no need to panic. Our overall supervisor phoned us about half past ten telling us that we should disband work and go home. We told him there was no more transport to take us to town and that he should come and pick us up. He told us he was already on his way home and that we had to find our way home. There was nothing else we could do about it. Brian stayed in Glenview, in the Western suburbs of Harare. I stayed in Chitungwiza which is about twenty five kilometres from Harare City Centre. We were on the other side of Harare City Centre, some fifteen kilometres or so from the city centre. We had to walk since public transport had since grounded for the day.

We winded through the winding streets, roads, and suburbs of Harare North on our way to Harare City Centre. It was at about half one in the afternoon when we reached the city centre. We tried to enter it through the northerly side but it was closed by the Riot police, with the help of the Army. So, we circled the city, and touched the western fringes of the city in the Belvedere area, then into the industrial areas of Workington, and then circled through Mbare Township. In Mbare we parted with Brian, him taking Simon Mazorodze Road to Glenview in that south westerly direction, and me crossing over into the Sunningdale area until I reached Seke road, to the south of Harare. So, I joined the other workers still treading this road on their way to Chitungwiza. I walked for closer to ten kilometres in this road until at about Manyame Airbase turnoff. With the group I was walking with we managed to force some small truck to take us to Chitungwiza. We had to stand in the middle of the road, wielding stones and boulders of rocks. We told him to stop the truck and that he should pick us or else we were going to stone him and his car. He stopped and agreed to take us to Chitungwiza. We were lucky. Some people had to complete the journey on foot. The half-ton truck was packed to spilling. We were 35 of us packed in that truck. He delivered us to our homes without even getting paid for the service.

The morrow day the Trade Unions said the strike was continuing until the government agreed to force the shop owners to reduce prices of their goods. That's why the country had gone on a nationwide strike, to force the government to curtail the prices of basic commodities that were skyrocketing. The Trade Unions were at the fore front of organizing this strike. I didn't even attempt going to the workplace, or even anywhere else that day for I was still nursing my painful legs and feet.

Some buses that were still plying the route to Harare were burned down. The road to Harare was blocked by large boulders of rocks. Up to now, these boulders of rocks still litter the roadsides. I have wondered a lot over the years where they could have got those rocks and how they transported them into the roads. The shops were broken into. For some biggest part of that day I stood aside watching and refused to enter this breaking into shops, vandalising and looting of the shops. As the day wore on and when it became obvious that every shop at this shopping centre was going to be vandalised I realised that if I couldn't join those hordes of people who were breaking into shops and get some food and store some of the food I was going to starve the following weeks because they wouldn't be anything in the shops to buy after the strike. Let alone, the majority of shop owners would be repairing their shops. So, at about night's fall I entered into this madness. Into night's fall almost everyone had entered into this madness. It was so hilarious and funny the moment you get into the spirit of it. It was also liberating. We collected as much of food as was possible and hide it in the sports grounds of a nearby school where we knew nobody could find it, if our homes were going to be searched. At one point people cheered me as I grabbed and run with a full thigh of the cow, which we roasted as braai and biltong meat throughout the night. We didn't sleep

174

that night, not a lot of people slept that night. Everyone was waiting for the chance to break into a particular shop at this shopping centre that hadn't been breached.

The Army and Police managed to secure the shop. They were walking around the shop throughout the night, guarding it against vandalisation. They were armed with live ammunition. Some people slept a couple of metres away from this shop, lying to these police officers that they were afraid of violence if they were to sleep in their homes. The truth was they were waiting for a small chance to break into this shop and the shop belonged to a local politician. He had used his power, influence and money to force the police and army to stop guarding the whole suburb but to concentrate on his shop. The police did exactly that and hadn't left the shop for that entire night, and for the coming nights whilst people waited in vain, incensed. The people accused the government of conniving with these shop owners by allowing them to arbitrarily raise the prices of basic commodities. So, it was in this milieu, that the people hit back, at the shop owners, by vandalising their shops. It was happening throughout the country.

When the government realised that the strike would never end they deployed the fully armed soldiers into the streets. They were armed to the teeth, even with war artillery and machine guns on unarmed civilians. The government gave the army the right to use maximum force and declared a state of emergency. They even said it was now a war situation, that the soldiers were trained to kill, so they would kill anyone who continued striking. That everyone should return to work instantly and that those who wouldn't would face persecution. The soldiers killed a couple or so people for show. The strikers disbanded the strike and returned back to work. It was nearly a week when the strike stopped. We returned back to work, defeated. After that strike nothing really got back to real normal. The entire zoned-out workforce would fill their brains and stomachs with nothing, without asking questions of what went wrong with the food riots. The government wouldn't allow any more strikes and responded to any strike threat with instant force. The labour unions were caged by the government. Most shop owners, factories and whole industries folded in and things went to the dogs.

Chapter 17

Conditioned To Fear

Kanzura Katipedza: "Excuse me, people of Nyatate ward! We are gathered here specifically to hear the message from our Comrade MP, Wa Chirowangoto. But before we give him the stage we need to welcome him *mumusangano* (the Jongwe party) way. We ask the youths to lead us in the chanting of the slogans and some dances.

Komurade Hokoyoi: *Pamberi naMudhara wedu!* (Forward with our Old man, *the nick name given to the president of the Jongwe party*)

Povho: *Pamberi!* (Forward)

Kuomurade Hokoyoi: *Pamberi nemusangano!* (Forward with Jongwe party)

Povho: *Pamberi!* (Forward)

Komurade Hokoyoi: *Pamberi nokutora ivhu!* (Forward with the land grab)

Povho: *Pamberi!* (Forward)

Komurade Hokoyoi: *Pasi nevarungu!* (Down with the whites)

Povho: *Pasi navo!* (Down with them)

Komurade Hokoyoi: *Pasi nembwasungata!* (Down with the white apologists)

Povho: *Pasi nadzo!* (Down with them)

Komurade Hokoyoi: Pasi naTsungirirai imbwasungata! (Down with Tsungirira, a white apologist. *Tsungirirai is the president of DALP, the opposition party to Jongwe party*)

Povho: *Pasi naye!* (Down with him)

Komurade Hokoyoi: *Pasi nezvimbwasungata DALP!* (Down with white apologist, the DALP)

Povho: *Pasi nayo!* (Down with it)

Then he started the new war cry for Jongwe party, a song that praises Mudhara and the land reform he had carried out, how they took the land from the whites through war and force and how people had to continue being strong as the country experienced economic problems, resultant of the land reform exercise.

Mudhara murambe makashinga heree?
Shingirirai, gadzirirai, Zimbabwe ndeyedu.
Baba murambe makashinga, Zimbabwe ndeyedu.

Makashingaa,
Rambai makashinga.
Rambai makashinga.

makashingahee?
Rambai makashinga.
Makashingaa,
Rambai makashinga.
Baba murambe makashinga, Zimbabwe ndeyedu.

Ivhuirii?
Takaritora nehondo.

Takaritora nehondo.

Neshungu neshungu?
Ticharima neshungu.
Ticharima neshungu.

The Povho (the people) and young comrades danced as they sang the song in praise of Mudhara and the Jongwe party. Even the old ladies had to dance, despite the fact that they were old and hadn't eaten anything since the last night's supper, everyone had to dance, artificial appreciation was better than not doing anything. When the song had ended Kanzura Katipedza continued.

The above play script extract is from the play I have been writing on Zimbabwe, tentatively entitled, THE RAGE OF DEVILS. I took this extract because of the song in this extract. This song was used on the public broadcaster's stations, in political gatherings, in every facet of Zimbabwe at a level I can't even begin to explain, as a war cry by the ZANU-PF during the years it instituted a culture of fear in the entire country. At one time this song would be heard on the electronic media, every five or so minutes. There was no repose for anyone because they had programmed it in such that it was playing pretty much every time on the airwaves, in varying times, on ZBC's 4 radio stations, and 2 TV stations. We had nowhere to hide from it.

Makashingaa,
Rambai makashinga.
Rambai makashinga.

Especially these words became deeply embedded in our psyche. They meant,

stronger,
stay stronger,
stay stronger.

It was staying stronger against the country's meltdown, against the Western colonisers, against anything that was against the ZANU-PF party, against the MDC. It was exhorting the whole country to be stronger against all these. The MDC was made to be the enemy within, so it had to be crushed. Anyone against the ZANU-PF was termed an enemy, just like George Bush 'axis of evil' ideology, the MDC, NGOs, the Western nations, etc..., were looped together as enemies against the ZANU-PF and the country. The land reform that had been carried out had been done through forceful, killing, maiming, and victimisation of the whites. Since the year-2000 constitution referendum, which the government lost by 45 against the 55% No vote, the ZANU-PF government entered into a fear factor drive on the electorate.

People were killed, people disappeared in broad daylight, the opposition was victimised, activists in the opposition were killed, the MDC leadership were victimised, beaten, some killed like Learnmore Jongwe, the people were pushed from their homes, the people were told they had to support the ZANU-PF or risk killings, the independent newspapers were bombed and burned, its editors were victimised and beaten like Trevor Ncube, Jeff Nyarota etc... The ministry responsible for media, information and publicity, through the state broadcaster, became the propaganda mouth-piece of this drive to create fear in people's hearts. Jonathan Moyo, who was the minister then, and who is now the minister, made inflammatory speeches that encouraged militant ZANU-PF youths to use fear and victimisation to decapitate anyone who was against the ZANU-

PF and the country. He went about disputing everyone who said anything against the ZANU-PF, telling the whole nation that his, and only his view, was important in Zimbabwe. Border Gezi and Elliot Manyika, who were the ministers of youths and the political commissars of the ZANU-PF created militant youths that were used to victimise the citizens, and these killed with impunity. Elliot Manyika with Brain Muteji also sang a song of fear, saying that ZANU-PF stands for blood, and the country was won with blood, thus it can only be defended by blood alone. The state institutions for order and law were made redundancy, like the police and the justice system, by the politicisation of these institutions. The army was employed into the streets for any minor strike against this government, and machine guns were patrolling the streets, the helicopters flying above the town's skies, instilling fear. We were cowed, we were butchered, we were preyed, we were told to keep quiet, and we were told to support the ZANU-PF or incur the worse. It reminded me of the experiment by Pavlov, the Pavlovian theory, or classical conditioning theory that we covered in our consumer buyer behaviour course, in the marketing diploma, offered by the *Southern African Institute of Marketing*. We were studying the concept of learning.

The ZANU-PF used the same theory and concepts to create, or make us learn about the culture of fear. This learning goes back to pre-independence era. Even during the liberation war, people were made to fear this party, and the Rhodesian white supremacist government did the same, too. Those who were found to be against the liberation cause were killed, as well as those who were against the white supremacist government. Even when you didn't do anything to help any of the two competing sides, you were killed. By just being a Zimbabwean, you were an enemy and were killed. This happened again in the Matabeleland Gukurahundi, where people were killed for no apparent reason, at all, but just because they stayed in the areas the rebels were working from.

Through the massive killings, displacements, and maiming of the Matabeleland people, in which over 20 000 were said to have been killed; they created the culture of fear. Through all these actions we became refugees in our own homes, in our own person. We become afraid of ourselves, because this *ourselves* was capable of creating danger on ourselves. We watered down this *ourselves*, we disobeyed this *ourselves*. Even when we were inside four walls we were not safe from ourselves. We were made into prey by the ZANU-PF

In, THE ANATOMY OF POLITICAL PREDATION (2011: 5) Bratton and Masunungure defines political predation saying,

> With reference to Nigeria under the Babangida dictatorship, Peter Lewis (1996) defines predatory rule as "a personalistic regime ruling through coercion and material inducement…that tends to degrade the institutional foundations of the state as well as the economy." Robert Fatton (1992) adds that predatory power relations have cultural as well as material roots. He depicts ruling classes in Africa as predatory in that they seek hegemony – meaning all-embracing social domination – over subordinate groups, whose political passivity is an element in their own oppression. We believe that, to apply well to Zimbabwe, the concept of political predation must also include the proclivity of leaders to unleash violence against (to "prey" upon) their own people. In other words, a predatory leadership not only fails to deliver developmental outcomes; it also kills, maims and terrorises its citizens. In this regard, Alnaswari's depiction of predatory rule in Iraq under Saddam Hussein is more apropos for Zimbabwe, where "the ruling group became preoccupied with its own survival" and employed "conspiracies, purges and counter purges, violent seizure of power and ruthless suppression of dissent" (2000, 2-3). In,

'When Things Fell Apart: State Failure in Late-Century Africa (2009)', Robert Bates argues that institutional and development outcomes depend on how ruling elites – whom he characterises as 'specialists in violence' – employ instruments of coercion to extract wealth from society. When the elite's political and economic interests are served by taxing production, they will establish the infrastructure of lawful state. If, however, they conclude that the costs of providing protection to society's producers outweigh the expected benefits, then they will be tempted to turn the state apparatus into an instrument of violent predation."

I will use the concepts of learning to analyse how the culture of fear and preyness was acculturated in our psyche. Learning is a process by which individuals acquire something, or knowledge of something and the experience to apply to a future-related behaviour. It may be accidental or intentional. The following learning elements helps the process of learning, motivations (based on goals and needs of the learner); cues (these are stimuli that gives direction to motives, like the above song being played several times on the radio); response (is the behaviour or reaction to a drive). The learner's response can be overt (observable) and non-overt (unobservable). Re-enforcement refers to anything that increases the likelihood of a specific response in future. There are 4 theories to learning.

The first one is Cognitive Learning Theory. This is learning based on mental activity by acquiring information from written and oral communication, through rote-memorisation and problem solving. The ZANU-PF machine made available, a lot of information to the people, information of hate against the above noted enemies against its rule. Through songs, through programmes on the radio and TV, through public gatherings, through music festivals, through newspapers; we were bombed with so much information. We had to learn through problem solving, mostly how to behave against the MDC and the other enemies of the ZANU-PF. Even when we didn't want to, we crammed this information through rote-memorisation. It was like an open university of fear. Through all that we learned about the culture of fear the ZANU-PF was instituting through this massive and all-pervasive information.

The second way we can learn is through modelling. This is when we can learn by observing others. When we observed our friend's relatives, colleagues etc..., getting victimised, killed, maimed, abused we learned the danger of disobeying ZANU-PF. Psychologist Neal E Miller and John Dollard calls this type of learning as imitative or imitation behaviour. Thus for us to avoid this victimisation we learned not to provoke that which caused this on us, our relatives, friends, colleagues. We learned to fear the instigator. Those who got something good from supporting the ZANU-PF, we imitated them. The opposition party and support of it was considered as selling the country to the imperialist. Masunungure observes,

> In Zimbabwe in the 1990s this official discourse was cast not only in the language of anti-imperialism but, increasingly with the racist charge that political opposition was tantamount to support for the restoration of white settler colonialism. Add to that the leadership's systematic plan to construct a politicized party-state and the question of alternation in power, or transfer of power from one party to another, does not arise (2004, 149).

We were told Mugabe is our messiah, so we learned to be like him, to make him our role-model, so that we would become like him, and thus we will be awarded by this system for modelling ourselves to the ZANU-PF or Mugabe. People in the ZANU-PF became our role-models, and a lot of us took to the ideology of this party, looking for benefits from this party, to be part of the system. The ZANU-PF party used both good modelling and bad modelling traits to create learning in us, by reward and punishment.

The third learning theory is Classical Conditioning that I have noted before. It was developed by the Russian psychologist, Ivan Petrovich Pavlov. I am sure a lot of us know of the Pavlov dog. He harnessed his dog and gave it powder meat whilst harnessed and observed that every time the dog would salivate and this was not learning, it was inherited reflex. Next, he started ringing a bell before feeding, repeating the sequence several times. And then next, he would ring the bell without giving the dog meat powder, and it salivated. The dog had been conditioned to salivate by the bell. The Pavlovian theory contented that if stimulus is paired with another stimulus that elicits a known response, and then the use of one stimulus serves to produce the same response when used alone. The learning occurred after the continuous pairings of meat powder and the bell, eventually when the bell alone was sounded, this caused the dog to salivate. The dog associated the bell (conditioned stimulus) with the meat powder (unconditioned stimulus), hence it gave the same response of salivation (unconditioned response) to the bell alone.

There are several instances the ZANU-PF used concepts of this theory to create the culture of fear. For instance the ZANU-PF would award people who would support it; things like food during draught years, agricultural implements, project monies etc. They associated this with support of the ZANU-PF. The ZANU-PF was the unconditioned response. These gifts given for obeying the party became the meat in Pavlov's experiment. These gifts should have been things that people should have been given without expecting them to support the ZANU-PF (unconditioned stimulus), but through this process people were made to know that through their support of the ZANU-PF, they would get their meat. This was fear of not getting the reward became the bell in Pavlov (conditioned stimulus). Thus through this we became the dogs of Pavlov,

185

but in this instance we were dogs of the ZANU-PF. This worked well in the situation because we were going through unprecedented financial, economic, social and political meltdown, where we were struggling everyday to survive. We were taught we had to listen to the fear inside us, fear that not supporting the ZANU-PF was sure going to be our demise. We learned to support it, even though we didn't want to. It was survival, and instinctual.

The first most important concepts of classical conditioning is repetition (this increases the strength of the association and slows the process of forgetting). This was used well through massive airplay given to ZANU-PF songs and programmes on the media. It got to be so excessive that it adversely affected retention and attention. We ended up avoiding these broadcasts on the public media, by resorting to foreign Medias. I also noted, we started by hating the song above. We would disdain the ZANU-PF, in our privacy, of abusing us through the overplaying and overhearing of this song on the media. Later on, even though we still didn't like it, we sort of could drift into singing the song. It was unconscious reflex. This is the conditioning we had been made to go through, through this excessive repetition, such that we ended up responding to the song, and I am sure, to the party.

The second concept of classical conditioning theory is through stimulus generalisation (classical conditioning theorists also say learning is possible through generalisation, which occurs when individuals give the same response to slightly different stimulus). When we used to be not afraid of our police force, before the military was deployed, and once we underwent harsh treatment at the hands of the military, ever after that the police, with its militarisation and politicisation was just as fearsome as the military. We now generally associated them with the military.

The third way is through stimulus discrimination (this concept is the opposite of stimulus generalisation. It essentially is the learner's ability to discriminate among stimuli). Through this concept we learned to discriminate between what really was the truth and just things put on us to create fear. Thus we learned to unlearn what the ZANU-PF was teaching us, by learning new things to counter to this. This formed the basis of our alignment towards the MDC.

The last theory of learning I want to explore in this culture of fear learning process we went through is Instrumental Conditioning. This was put in place by an American psychologist, B. F. Skinner. According to Skinner most individuals learn in a controlled environment, in which individuals are rewarded for choosing appropriate behaviour, like Pavlov, Skinner used animals for his experiment. He took some rats and placed them in a maze and immediately rewarded those that found their way out of the maze. This reward system was instrumental in teaching the rats to repeat the same behaviour and receive some food. The instrumental or *operant* conditioning theory suggests that learners learn by means of trial and error, in which some acquired behaviour result in favourable experiences, thus is instrumental in teaching the individual to repeat the specific behaviour.

We were put in a maze. We were told or made to realise we will be killed or abused if we don't subscribe to ZANU-PF ideologies. This was the maze. Those who found their way out of the maze, I mean those who believed in this ideology of the ZANU-PF and embraced the ZANU-PF became the mice that had found its way out of the maze, thus were awarded. People who had been huge critics of the ZANU-PF and Mugabe started supporting Mugabe, and thus they were richly awarded. Those who continued defying him were kept in the maze, a maze of killings, victimisations, abuse, maiming, a maze of fear. Thus we learned the importance of fear in conditioning us into supporting this party

I am not saying it's only us, the general people, who were made to learn about fear, and embraced fear as a limiting force in our political participations and activities. Even leaders in the opposition, especially Tsvangirai, who faced two treason trials, three murder attempts, and countless beatings was conditioned to fear. The turning point of this conditioning happened in the 2007 Save Zimbabwe prayers and activism in the Highfields suburb.

In a landmark event on March 11, 2007 the police prevented the Save Zimbabwe Campaign (a coalition of church and civic groups) from convening a "prayer meeting" in a residential area of Harare. Leaders of the opposition, including Morgan Tsvangirai, were brutally assaulted; one person was killed; 50 were hospitalised; and nearly 200 were arrested. Media coverage of these events evoked an international outcry, not only from the governments of Great Britain, the European Union and the United States, but also from the African Commission on Human and People's Rights. Internally, the Catholic Bishops issued a pastoral letter asserting that "black Zimbabweans today fight for the same basic rights they fought for during the liberation struggle." Mugabe's reaction to this criticism was to announce: 'If they (protest) again, we will bash them' Bratton and Masunungure (2011:29).

I remember what Mugabe said when he was asked why Tsvangirai was beaten. In the initial mêlée, Tsvangirai had been spared the violence when his aides removed him from the place of the prayers before the abuse started. When his colleagues were arrested, the likes of Lovemore Madhuku, he went to the police station to voice his displeasure at their continuing incarceration in the police cells. This is where he was beaten, not in the actual protest. He was beaten to a pulp for asking that they be released. When Mugabe was asked why Tsvangirai was beaten. He said he deserved the beating. That he had no right to go to the police station to ask or protest, and that he was seeking for such a beating. He said since the police specialised in this (had *degrees in violence*) they were simply doing their job. He even promised Tsvangirai he would be thrashed, even a lot harder if he were to go back to the police station, again. He claimed proudly that the ZANU-PF had *degrees in violence*, and would use it at any dissent against its rule.

Ever after this we stopped protesting against the ZANU-PF, we watered down, we became meek. We were always afraid of the ZANU-PF. We were overwhelmed in fear. We had learned our lessons.

Chapter 18

Unlearning Fear: The Shadow That Refused To Leave

I remember when we were growing up; it was my big brother's favourite story. Every time we narrated tales to each other at home he always told this story, and he would vary it, a bit in every telling, but the gist of the story was the same as below:

There were the two of them, herding cattle. There were now looking for their husbandry, some had wondered into Chitsoko Forest. There were in the dark fringes of this superstitiously, darkly endowed forest, Chitsoko Forest, to the east of their homesteads, near the more superstitious Nyanga Mountains. The area where their cattle had meandered into had a story, always whispers with omens, dark stories. A couple of years before two boys who were herding their goats had tried to enter it to take their goats, and they were swallowed by Waraza, the spirit medium of this area, who was said to be in homage, in Nyanga Mountain and would sometimes come into Chitsoko Forest, hunting for people to take into its embodiment. Some said the boys had said things disrespectful to this place. People were not allowed to say anything when they enter this place, or think little of anything in this place, even ants and flies were sacred in this place, and had to be respected. Even after the family of those boys had done an appeasement ceremony to recover their boys, Waraza refused to release them; they were now parts of this spirit medium. The family eventually had to accept that they had lost their children to Waraza. This was what a lot of villagers were afraid of, having their children taken by this spirit medium, and this is what these two boys, Zvaitwa and Chamunoda were afraid of. They cursed themselves for letting the cattle wonder into

Chitsoko as they played. They were so scared. In spring, this was also the only place still abundant with graze for the cattle, so they had grazed their cattle near this place. It was also the devil they knew how to deal with; they simply had to be respectful of the place, so they hugged this forest as they look for their husbandry.

It was late afternoon when the sun begins to redden the western horizons, and colours the things with shadows, light, beautiful, sometimes crazy shadows, dark. It was in late October, and the two were rounding their cattle before they were really swallowed by the forest, to take home. And then Zvaitwa noticed, as if for the first time, some unexplained thing on him. At first he told himself he had always known this thing on him, but the crazy forest whispered something else into his mind. It seemed it was the first time he had noticed it. Zvaitwa thought it was just his mind that was doing this trick on him, or had his eyes become starry eyed. So, he shook himself, and tried to focus again on the thing, and then he bellowed in fear, calling his brother Chamunoda who was just across the river, Chitsoko River, to come over, to rush to his abidance, to his defence. In a very high voice he pleaded with his brother.

"Chamunoda, please rush over here. There is some dark thing that is attached to me, please rush Chamunoda before it takes me, please rush before Waraza takes me away with her...please, please..."

"What thing. What thing Zvaitwa, I am rushing over. I am coming straight away, so don't be afraid, brother."

Chamunoda had to swim through Chitsoko River, through a very deep pool, that was said to have crocodiles but he wasn't afraid. He knew he had to make it as soon as possible to prise his brother away from the grip of Waraza. He would do anything to please and satisfy Waraza so that she could let go off her brother. Finding a narrow crossing point across this river would have delayed him. It was even better to lose all the livestock into the gulp of Chitsoko Forest than to lose his brother, so he had abandoned them in his rush. He found his younger brother wilting away from some unnoticeable thing, hugging himself to the ground, shivering, whimpering, watching the ground close to himself for this something.

"Where is the spirit medium, Zvaitwa?"

His brother could only nod his head towards the ground, pointing with his eyes, now afraid of using his hands or fingers. Chamunoda followed the direction of his brother's nodding, and then he saw it. He thought he knew it, but was surprised he had never really noticed it on him or on his brother. In that split moment he told himself it was something not to be afraid of, or was it something to be afraid of? Was it that dangerous? He shivered as he checked himself to figure out whether things were different with him. Then he saw it, too. It was on him, and he thought, at first, it was a joke so he moved a bit, and then it followed him. For the first time he was so afraid. He started shouting some angry scared expletives at it, telling it to leave him alone, but it shouted back at him in his scared voice, and refused to leave him. He told his brother.

"Let's go and swim in the river. Maybe we can cleanse it out of us through swimming."

So, the two rushed into the river. The river was a bit muddy so they couldn't see those two things after a few dives and cleansing efforts. They scrubbed themselves in this river, until they were a burning brown and when they felt they had cleansed these out of themselves they came out of the river, only to find that the shadows had re-attached to them again. Then Zvaitwa mused loudly.

"Chamunoda, I think we can sort of give these things some food to eat. Maybe they don't want to leave us because they are hungry. So, let's give them our share of food, maybe they won't eat us if they are satisfied with the delicious food we have."

So the two rushed back to their food bags, took the very best food, pieces of soft tasty beef of a young calf they had slaughtered a couple of days before, and Sadza (a thickened porridge made of maize flour), which they threw at their shadows, telling them, cajoling them.

"This is the food we have. Please eat it and leave us alone."

Zvaitwa said this, but the shadows didn't reply him, neither did they eat anything of the food they were given. Exasperated with this behaviour, Chamunoda enthused.

"Maybe their throats are dry and thirsty, so let's give them drinking water to moisten their throats."

"Maybe we could do that", Zvaitwa agreed.

The two rushed to the river, got a good mouth-full of water from the river and pissed it onto their shadows, which their shadows drunk, but kept demanding for more, quietly. So, these two brothers went back to the river to fetch more, and more water, which they gave to their shadows, but their shadows refused to leave them, unquenched. The two boys got desperate and angry as they kept offering these shadows water and many other things to prise them off their bodies. So, they decided, silently to each other, so that these shadows won't hear them, to castrate them, to beat up these ungrateful things. They got themselves some big branches of Mupotanzou tree, which was very good for this task. And so, they started by warning these ungrateful things of what awaits them.

"We are going to beat the crap out of you if you don't leave us out of your own free will. We are sick and tired of you; you ungrateful things! We have given you everything but you are still demanding and demanding. We can't keep up with this greedy behaviour of yours", said Chamunoda, and Zvaitwa concurred with his brother.

"Yes, you are very ungrateful bastards. We have given you all the best, but you don't want to leave us alone, so we will castrate you to teach you a good lesson, to be grateful." But their shadows could only repeat after them, thereby infuriating these two brothers, all the more.

"You think you are great."

"You think you are great." Their shadows responded after them.

"You are stupid."

"You are stupid", their shadows insulted them, as well.

"We are going to have to kill you."

"We are going to have to kill you", their shadows threatened, too.

The brothers looked at each other; their shadows did the same, too. The boys were scared but they concurred through looks and raised their big sticks, so did their shadows. They raised them higher and higher and their shadows did the same thing, too. Then the two boys stopped and their shadows stopped, too. They looked at each other and agreed to give their shadows one hell of a wallop, and they started downing their sticks onto their shadows and their shadows did the same. The boys threw their sticks away, afraid of the beating they were going to receive as complimentary from their shadows. They started running for home, leaving everything including their husbandry. They were shouting, crying, haloing, at the top of their voices, and their shadows followed suit, too. They ran without resting for nearly fifteen kilometres to their homesteads, and arrived home amid these hullabaloos.

When they arrived home, they let their parents and the villagers know what was the matter with them, and it created some more confusion. On every one of this little village, and it grew into the next villages, when they started realising they had been spooked by these things, as well. Some people accused these two boys of bringing such misfortune to them; some started concocting measures to deal with these unknowns. Some people suggested that they were evil spirits, so they pushed for the cleansing of an entire village, which they did, and these things refused to leave. Some did some other ceremonies, and it didn't help. Some bathed themselves, scrubbed themselves, until they were blue. Some people started, slowly started, to realise that these things were a part of them, that there was no way they were going to untouched themselves from these beings. It was an old man, from a distant village who started putting this idea into being when he said.

"These are part of us. There are an Us who will always be there with us as long as we live. No matter how much we do to do away with it, we will never walk away from this being because it is us. The only way we could walk away from this Us is through our own deaths." Some initiate to this idea asked,

"Where will they go when we die?"

"When we die this flesh is going to decay in the soils, and eventually the bones too, but these Us will never die nor decay. They will go to a spiritual home. They are our spirits, and I suppose we will be these things when we die." The old man tried to understand it that way.

And for some people of this village, and others, it began to make sense as they tried to grapple with this old man's wise words. It was difficult, but it made sense somehow. As they accepted and tried to live peacefully with these things, the more they began to feel at home with themselves again, the way they were before this discovery.

That's definitely a silly story; fantasy or folklore story, and I know the squares are bothered. Knives have been drawn out. One critic, in my previous non-fiction book, ZIMBABWE: THE BLAME GAME said I should only write fiction, or if I want to write non-fiction I should respect the rules of non-fiction writing. I couldn't answer her, and I feel the only way a writer can answer well the critics is by continuing doing the thing he feels he is right in doing that. I have never been a rules sort of person, so I am not going to follow rules particularly, as you have discovered, reading the rest of the book. This folkloric story deals with the issues I want to be dealing with in this topic, that's why it is here.

I think there are a lot of theories on how one can move away from his shadow I have heard. Dambudzo Marechera, in his novel, THE BLACK INSIDER, has a take at it, as well. He talks of how the film people use the photographic effect to create this illusion, whereby the light is focused on a white curtain with the character standing behind this curtain, for some time. When people are conditioned to observing the same character at the same spot, and when the character moves, the people would still see him there, but it will be his illusion or shadow. In that moment, Marechera said, the character could have walked away from his shadow. The shadow stays a bit, until the watchers' eyes have adapted to the absence of the character and the shadow. Oliver Mtukudzi, a famous Zimbabwean folklorist singer uses this idea of walking away from shadows in his song; saying, when are you going to stop running away from your shadow, that you should be in step with your shadow, come to terms with it. This is what I am trying to focus with the story, as well. How we can come to confront our shadows and come to terms with them?

I want to take the shadows in the story as the fear of or Mugabe in the Zimbabwean political issues context. Though the characters in the story didn't create their shadows, it was there all along, but it was their recognition of these shadows that they started creating these shadows. It is in our creation of Mugabe that we began to understand the fear that he was capable of inflicting on us. It is us who created Mugabe. We allowed him a lot of leeway to abuse us without questioning him. It started before independence, but then we had little control over him, but the biggest formative years of this Mugabe we were creating happened in the Gukurahundi massacres, where the biggest part of the country and the international community kept a blind eye on him. It was the shadow that we had, we knew we had it on us, but we never really saw it, thus unconsciously we started creating it, making it grow on us until when in the 1990s we started seeing this shadow, as if for the first time. We started trying to run away from it, at first we didn't really do so with a lot of conviction because we thought it could be leaving us alone as soon as was possible. We thought it could do so the moment it started realising we didn't want it on us. But, we discovered this shadow was deeply embedded in us. Like the characters in the above story we tried every method to delete this Mugabe on us. But, this shadow, in failing to delete it; piled up some more fear on us. Mugabe did the same with us. The more we tried to do away with him, the more he piled more fear on us, the more he hurt us. Did he hurt us because he was afraid of us, no, he hurt us because we were afraid of ourselves that we saw in him.

So, we have been on this road for a long, long time, and the shadow is still on us. This shadow, this fear is us. This is what we have to recognise first for us to start the process towards unlearning fear again. That this fear is deeply embedded in us and we can only deal with it by accepting it as part of us, because it influences us every day. We can no longer hate it but love it, and try to now make it part of who we will be in the future.

Mugabe or the fear of him is going to define us, to help us unlearn not to trust ourselves. We can develop better attitudes towards fear in order to change attitudes against fear. I am going to use attitudes theories to figure out how we can deal with fear.

Attitude is a learned predisposition to behave in a consistently favourable or unfavourable way with respect to a given object. From the definition, it brings out the following, 1) there has to be an attitude object (Mugabe or fear of Mugabe, or even fear of us), that is that thing or things in a thing that makes us start having attitudes for or against it, 2) attitudes are a learned predisposition, which we can do using the learning concepts I have dealt with in the essay CONDITIONED TO FEAR above, 3) attitudes have consistency, that is, attitudes are consistent with the behaviour they reflect, 4) attitudes occur within a situation, that is, attitudes are related to the events or circumstances at any given point in time.

These are the strategies towards change. The first strategy of attitude change is by changing the basic motivational function by making new needs more prominent. The following are the 4 functional approaches to motivational function: A) Utilitarian function involves changing attitudes through showing the functions or tasks or utility that an object can produce. Obviously there are things (functions, tasks, utility) both good and bad that Mugabe, or fear of him has achieved with us. For example, as I have noted before he did great things with our education system. This is one of the good utility or function he could have executed that well. We can emphasise this to deal with the fear of him as a monster. Even the fear can work as function, as well. It should be helping us push some more towards freedom, rather than freezing us.

B) ego-defensive function is whereby attitudes can be changed through the person's self-image from inner feelings of uncertainty or doubt. This is where our biggest problem is centred on, uncertainty and doubt. We now doubt even ourselves because he made us doubt ourselves. We doubt we are capable of not creating trouble for ourselves. We doubt what we believe in. We are uncertain of the future, if we were to choose anything else..., we have to burrow down inside us and try to find who really we are and what we really believe in, and do that, despite the fact that they will be a part of us that would doubt us.

C) Value-expressive function is whereby attitudes are reflections of the person's general values and life styles, and then you can come up with qualities of an object that are aligned to those values. I have this huge conviction that whatever Mugabe is, is our construction, sometimes not willingly so we constructed him. He comes from two important worlds, the traditional African society or civilisation. It is the same world that would tell us not to question our adult decisions, it is the system that believed some people were more important than others, it was the system of kingship or monarchs, thus of governance that were undemocratic. As the outside systems started filtering into our societies we started questioning and problematizing our system, and question our elders and leaders. It was a response to the limiting aspects of our old system that created leaders like Mugabe who would institute fear in us.

The other world is of the Western/catholic system. The Catholic Church, for a long time here, has been about centralising power in a few individuals. I want to talk of my parish. For some years power had been centred on a few individuals, with some leaders staying in executives for in excess of 10 years without having to go through any elective system, and the rest would complain about that without recourse. Some few years ago there was change in the Vicarage, and the new priests we were given brought very marked changes. They instituted a system whereby leadership of the church, in its various facets, had to change every two years through elections. The old people who had been used to the semi-monarchy leadership system, who were the very people who had started the church, and were the same people who would rule or control the church in the old system, became disillusioned with these new changes. Mugabe grew up in the catholic framework, and he still is a catholic, and I suppose these leadership problems of the Catholic Church influenced his styles. The change in the system in the Catholic Church here could be a direct response to the Mugabe and fear culture he instituted on us. The church leaders may have realised their systems were breeding grounds to create leaders like Mugabe. This is evidenced by the fact that the Catholic Church, especially its bishops, they are now huge critics of Mugabe. Back, in the first two decades of Mugabe's leadership, pretty much the same bishops, with a few exceptions like Pius Ncube, were huge proponents of the same person.

D) Knowledge function is whereby people who have a high need for cognition, need to know about anything around them.

We can deal with the issue of Mugabe and fear he has instituted in us by accessing more information on him, trying to understand him, trying to understand the fear in us. Knowledge has the ability to open up frontiers.

The second strategy of attitude change is by associating the attitude object with a specific group or event. For instance we can associate Mugabe with the school of politicians, who exercise leadership through force, or leaders who favours nationalistic ideologies, or proud leaders. We can get to terms with him when he expresses himself in these tendencies, or we can easily figure out a way to subvert these tendencies because we already understand where he is coming from. We learn to understand the fear he will be unleashing on us, it is our fear of him.

The third strategy is whereby we will resolve two conflicting attitudes. We can make ourselves aware that this attitude we have towards fear is in conflict with our other important attitude toward freedom of expression thus we learn to value this fear by resolving its conflictions with freedom of expression.

The fourth strategy is of altering the components of the multi-attribute model. This model portrays a person's attitude with regard to an attitude object as a function of one's perceptions and assessment of the key attributes or beliefs held with regard to a particular object. The following multi-attribute model components are the ones we focus on and change or work around with, that is, 1) we measure attitudes towards an object or person by evaluating the specific beliefs and attributes of this object, 2) we focuses attention on attitudes towards behaviour or acting with respect to an attitude object, 3) we do a comprehensive integration of the attitude components into a structure that is designed to lead to both better explanations and better predictions of behaviour. In this we also incorporate the other models of attitude formation like the tri-component models, 4) we account for the many cases where the action or outcome is not certain but instead reflects the person's attempts to develop an attitude, 5) we highlight how exposure to information especially though advertisement or some promotional vehicles would affect a person's attitude towards a particular object.

Attitude change can also be done by changing the relative evaluation of attitudes, changing the beliefs against the object, and adding and removing an attribute.

Change is always important in trying to heal ourselves in every aspect, disease, or behaviour. The most important aspect about these is if we are not open to change, most likely these things will only be rectified through our deletion, death, like the characters in the above story came to accept the only way the shadows could leave them was through their death. So, it is important that we embrace change for that change to shape us or heal us. To live is a choice. Fear can be changed by willing to live again, and to embrace change.

References

Alnasrawi, A. (2000). 'Iraq: Economic Embargo and Predatory Rule' in E. Nafziger; F. Stewart; and R. Vayrynen (eds.) *War, Hunger and Displacement: The Origins of Humanitarian Emergencies,* Oxford University Press, vol. 2 pp. 89-119, Oxford.

Bates, R. (2009). *When Things Fell Apart: State Failure in Late-Century Africa,* Cambridge University Press, New York.

Beetham, D. (1999). *Democracy and Human Rights,* Polity Press, Cambridge.

Bratton, M and Masunungure, E. (2011) *Anatomy of Political Predation: Leaders, Elites and Coalitions in Zimbabwe, 1980-2010,* Research paper 09, Developmental Leadership Program, Online.

Chan, S. (2008). *The Tragedy of Morgan Tsvangirai,* Prospect, Issue 149.

Chitiyo, K. (2009). *A Case for Security Sector Reform in Zimbabwe,* Royal United Services Institute, occasional paper edited by Anna Rader and Adrian Johnson http://www.rusi.org.

Dzinesa, G. A. and Zambara, W. (undated). *SADC's Role in Zimbabwe: Guarantor of Deadlock or Democracy,* Academic article, Online.

Fatton, R. (1992). *State and Civil Society in Africa,* Lynne Reinner Publishers, Boulder, Colorado.

Hamill, J. (2008). *National unity option is a dead end,* The Guardian, 3 July 2008.

Lewis, P. (1996). *From Prebendalism to Predation: The Political Economy of Decline in Nigeria,* Journal of Modern African Studies, 34 (1) pp. 79-103.

Mandaza, I (ed.) (1986). *Zimbabwe: The Political Economy of Transition, 1980-1986,* CODESRIA, Dakar.

Mapuva, J. (2010). *Government of National Unity(GNU) as a Conflict Prevention Strategy: Case of Zimbabwe and Kenya.* Journal of Sustainable Development in Africa Volume 12, No.6, Clarion University of Pennsylvania, Clarion, Pennsylvania.

Marcantoni, J (ed.) and Oliver, Z. M (ed.) (2013). *There is No Cholera in Zimbabwe,* Aignos Publishing Inc, Honolulu, Hawaii.

Masunungure, E. (2004). Travails of Opposition Politics in Zimbabwe Since Independence, in David Harold-Barry (ed.) *Zimbabwe: The Past Is the Future,* Weaver Press pp. 147-192, Harare.

Maunganidze, O.A. (2009). *Post-Election Power-Sharing Governments and the Future of Democracy in Africa,* Institute for Security Studies, Pretoria.

Saed, M.A. (2010). *From Conventional Peace-building Paradigms in Post-Conflict Settings and Reconstruction to Systemic Multi-Foci Approaches: The Case of Somaliland,* Retrieved from: http://www.monitor.upeace.org/innerpg.cfm?id_article=7 25#_ftnref2.

Zimbabwe Election Support Network. (2012). *BALLOT UPDATE,* Issue 9: September to October 2012.

Printed in the United States
By Bookmasters